BLACK LAKE

About George Galloway

George Galloway was a Member of the British Parliament for nearly 30 years. He is a TV and radio broadcaster, a filmmaker and writer. He is a father of six and lives with his young family in rural Scotland.

Also by George galloway

Downfall: The Ceaucescus and the Romanian Revolution
(1991)

I'm Not The Only One (2004)

Mr Galloway Goes to Washington (2005)

Fidel Castro Handbook (2006)

Open Season (2011)

The Quotable Galloway: From Alcohol to Zionism (2014)

Street Fighting: A Memoir of the 1970s (2017)

Queensway (2019)

Published by Molucca Media Ltd
49 Greek Street
London W1D 4EG

Printed by Book Empire
www.bookempire.co.uk
Unit 7, Lotherton Way, Garforth, Leeds, LS25 2JY

Printed in Great Britain

ISBN 978-1-9163153-2-7

BLACK LAKE

GEORGE GALLOWAY

Book Two in the Queensway series

molucca media ltd

broadcasting, publishing, film production & journalism

For

Òban Amaria

Prologue

The Queensway series recounts the invasion and gradual occupation of Great Britain by Nazi Germany.

The Dunkirk evacuation has failed, the gallant RAF has lost the Battle of Britain and the Royal Navy has been betrayed by key admirals. Hitler is here. His Nazi Party establishes its headquarters in Whiteleys, the department store in London's Bayswater. The whole area of Queensway is Nazi Central protected by an iron ring of the SS and British Fascist collaborators.

The abdicated pro-Nazi King Edward has been restored to the throne alongside his dominant, grasping American wife, the now Queen Wallis.

Sir Oswald Mosley is the Prime Minister in 10 Downing Street. But Mr Churchill has escaped and, from his hiding place in the South Wales valleys, is leading the resistance in the name of the rightful king, now safe with his family beyond the seas in the Dominions.

And the resistance packs an increasing punch...

1

August 1940. West Bromwich

No one really knew if there had ever been a lake. But if there had been, it would have been black. It wasn't called the Black Country for nothing. Two centuries of coal mining, iron ore extraction and hundreds of belching chimneys endlessly pumping black soot. The whole of the West Midlands constituted the workshop of the workshop of the world. But the Black Country was the blackest. Its people, too, were not quite, somehow, even English. Their unmistakable accents owing more to ancient Saxon than to the received pronunciation.

Though only a few miles away, Birmingham might have been Paris. And now, like Paris, they were all under Nazi occupation and the air was thick with Hunnish commands, the click of heels, the stomp of the jackboot.

After London, the industrial heartland, the second region of England, and the second city of the Empire had to be occupied next. And now it was. Whilst most of the rest of southern England was now lightly garrisoned with German, Romanian, Hungarian and Bulgarian units – second-rate troops all – Birmingham and the West Midlands was now tied down by an entire full-strength division of the Wehrmacht, backed by the SS and local quislings from the British Union of Fascists. The Prime Minister, Sir Oswald Mosley, was stronger here than anywhere else. His BUF was more than ten thousand strong across the West Midlands. The entire campus of the University of Birmingham was now a Nazi fortress

Black Lake was on the outskirts of West Bromwich and home to hundreds of ordnance workers mainly based in a huge Gothic building several miles away called Kenrick House, which assembled artillery shells by the tens of thousands every week. A battered omnibus brought the workforce back and forth each day between the crude, makeshift dwellings erected in the previous century and the 19th century Gothic horror of the factory. In addition to the housing, those less fortunate made do with caravans, some still horse-drawn. The majority of the workforce were Irish immigrants, the caravan people too.

Churchill's imprecations to war workers to sabotage their plants, to strike, to abscond and join the resistance had fallen on deaf ears on the Black Lake, not least amongst the Irish labourers. Churchill's role as Colonial Secretary was the reason, bringing in the Black and Tans, seeking to drown the Emerald Isle in Irish blood.

So when London fell the munitions factory hands continued to work for the war effort – on enhanced pay too – even their charge hand, Jim Coogan, a Scotsman of Irish descent. Even if the fruits of their labour were now to be plucked by enemy hands.

Coogan blew his whistle as he always did at bang on 8pm.

'Right, that's it for today, good work,' he said to each and every worker who passed him, or rather rushed past him on their way to the door and their bus.

It was not the end of the day for Coogan. As he moved around the now empty halls checking all machines were safely switched off he carefully checked the massive blackout curtains. It was a habit.

Obviously there were no Luftwaffe bombs raining down on the Midlands now, but Prime Minister Mosley had made clear the blackout must continue after rogue RAF fighters and bombers still loyal to the Crown had staged several attacks on railheads and vital infrastructure in several parts of the country, like electricity stations, including in the Midlands, before returning safely to their untamed fastness somewhere, Scotland perhaps, in the far north of the country.

His duties completed Coogan still did not go home. Sometimes he even slept in the factory.

He had no one to return to and not much of a home in any case. A renowned bagpiper and ceilidh organiser before the war, Coogan's heart lay in France, or rather with a French nurse from whom he hadn't heard since the fall of Paris. Sometimes he liked to imagine her as fighting with the Maquis, the French resistance. Although she was not a communist, as most of the Maquis were, she was a French patriot so passionate that she couldn't remain in England one minute longer once the Wehrmacht had stormed through the forest of the Ardennes and engaged French forces for the third time in seventy years. No amount of pleading from the nuns at the local Catholic charity hospital in which she was hugely popular, or from her lover Coogan, could keep her from returning home. Now, Coogan had no-one to play his pipes to.

He was not a communist either, and certainly not a British patriot. His allegiance was to the Irish Free State and de Valera. But he hated fascism with every fibre of his being. And he had been planning his next actions for many weeks.

At exactly midnight he opened the back door and, cupped in his hand, lit a cigarette. His match didn't show much light. But it was sufficient to signal to the houses opposite and more particularly to the shadowy figures sheltering in their lea that it was on, that the door was open.

Crossing the road crouched, but with shuffling speed, one by one the men entered silently past him and gathered in the hallway. He was disappointed that there were only four of them. There was a lot of ground to cover.

'Where are the rest of you,' Coogan asked, 'and what are your names?'

'You don't need to know our names Jock, and we're two men down, arrested today on suspicion,' replied the gruff, unshaven leader of the cell, from above his muffler and beneath his cap brim pulled down as far over his face as it could go. In truth, all Coogan could see in the half-light was his broken, uneven yellow teeth.

'We won't be able to cover it all with just the five of us, that's all I meant' said Coogan, lamely and a bit embarrassed by his amateurism. 'I'm sorry for asking your names,' he added, just to underscore his mistake.

'Well, we'd best get started then,' said the Muffler. 'Where's the stuff?'

Coogan led the men silently into the boiler room where six large canvas bags lay concealed behind the main boiler.

'A fucking dangerous place to store TNT,' said the Muffler.

'I-I-I...know,' said Coogan 'but there was nowhere else I could safely hide them,' he replied truthfully.

'How long have they been here,' asked the Muffler, looking anxious.

'Just since this morning, they came with the other deliveries. There was no warning about where I should store them,' he replied.

'Not the delivery man's responsibility,' said the Muffler 'In fact he wouldn't even have known what was in the bags. It's all need to know, you know' he paused, 'although, of course, you don't.'

Sensing the other man's embarrassment the Muffler eased the tension and slapped Coogan on the back. 'Anyway, thanks for your assistance. Just show us the way to go and you can fuck off home,' he said.

'No way.' replied Coogan. 'I'm in for a penny so I might as well be in for a pound. Besides, I know my way around here in the dark better than anyone in the place. And if it comes off right, they're going to know it was me and I will end up hanging from the beams by piano wire. So the only fucking off I will be doing is when this job is done.'

'OK mate,' said the Muffler. 'It's up to you. Let's get started.'

The three men, who still hadn't spoken, took a bag each and rejected Coogan's offer to assist them. Leading the way up the stone steps Coogan and the Muffler, all five men, climbed absolutely silently. Coogan could have sworn he could hear the hammer of his heartbeat.

Below each assembly line the silent men carefully placed three sticks of TNT. It turned out that there were fifty sticks in every bag so three hundred sticks of dynamite.

'What about the shell storage area,' asked Coogan. 'How many are we keeping back for there?'

The Muffler seemed to smile, his eyes crinkling, although the other three men laughed out loud, the only sound which had emanated from them the whole time.

'Don't be soft lad,' said the Muffler, 'we only need one stick of dynamite to blow up every shell in this building, but we will put in three in case any of these are damp squibs.

'Besides,' he added, 'the shells in here can be easily enough replaced. Unless we blow the whole fucking factory sky-high.'

Coogan again swallowed his embarrassment and silently cursed his naivety.

It took only a few minutes to sow the dynamite throughout both factory and the store. The Muffler then turned to the detonation plan.

'How long have we got between leaving here and the balloon going up,' asked Coogan. His motorbike stood outside and he hoped he'd be in the queue for the ferry to Liverpool by the time their handiwork woke every fucker in the West Midlands.

'We've got no time at all,' said the Muffler. 'We will be lucky if we get to the end of West Bromwich High Street.

'What?' gasped Coogan. 'What is this, a fucking suicide mission? Don't you have timers?'

The three other men laughed out loud again.

'I did tell you to fuck off home,' said the Muffler. 'Obviously we hope it won't be a suicide mission. But I tell you this, if it is, it's a helluva fucking way to go!'

'So, there's no timer. So how do you detonate this then?' said Coogan, his head now spinning.

'Petrol lad, just petrol. Now go and fetch it, be a good lad.'

'Go and help him lads,' ordered the Muffler and the three of them, the four musketeers and Coogan, duly filed down the stairs.

'How much do we need?' asked Coogan of the silent men. Silent they remained. They merely held up five fingers. That was all he was going to get from them.

Coogan looked at the big company clock on the stairs just in time to hear it chiming 1am.

Moments later five cans of petrol were laid at the feet of the Muffler.

'OK here's what we are going to do.' Turning to his three men he firmly ordered, 'You three fuck off back to rooms now, fast as you can.' Turning now to Coogan the Muffler asked 'That's your motorbike out the back, right?'

Coogan nodded, though not before wondering momentarily how he knew that.

'Ok, you get down now and start up the bike, open the gates, remove any obstruction. You and me are going to make a fast getaway out of here.'

All four men scampered down the stairs, three going out the front, Coogan going out the back. He climbed on his BSA, kicked it and it roared into life first thing. He could see no obstacle either in the yard or in the small side street leading down to the main road.

The Muffler, meanwhile, was making trails, thin lines of petrol going everywhere across the floors of the production lines and through the heavy roller doors leading into the weapons store. Then down the stairs right down to the back door. He lit a rag and just as the back door was slamming shut he tossed the rag onto the ground where it instantly connected to the thin line of petrol.

Within a second he was on the pillion and thumping Coogan's back, who needed no encouragement. Like a bat out of hell he raced through the gates, down the side street onto the main road. Just as he was realising he had no idea where they were going the first of the explosions nearly blasted them both out of their precarious enough saddles.

The residents of West Bromwich and beyond, far beyond, either fell out of bed or, if further away, merely leapt out of bed at the sound. Most thought they counted six huge explosions before what will forever be known as the big one. The exploding shell storage hall took the entire roof off the building, raining down debris for miles around. Those bold enough to venture outside or just to their windows reported a huge ball of orange fire, a kind of mushroom shape aglow with the intensity of a small sun. Some were blinded by the light, others merely scorched by the wave of searing heat which raced through West Bromwich almost as fast as two motorcyclists, one tic-tacking directions to the other through the streets of the town.

Before the sun came up, the SS and the Gestapo were already arriving by the truckload in the workers district of Black Lake. There would be no omnibus today.

He felt the pressure on his back, the change of position, and then, above the thrum of the engine, the words in his ear.

'Where are we going?'

'I don't know,' Coogan shouted over his right shoulder. 'Anywhere. Just away. My place?'

His thoughts weren't coherent. He felt a combustible mix of emotions, a sour fear mixed with soaring relief, that they had destroyed the works and not themselves in the course of it.

'Ok,' he heard from behind, accompanied by a tap on the shoulder.

His house, a two-bedroom back-to-back, was only a few minutes walk from the factory, but in his blind panic to get away he had dialled open the accelerator with his right hand and let rip, with no destination in mind, just to get as far away as possible. Now he realised that the longer they were out, exposed, the more likely they would be to be stopped, with no plausible explanation as to why two men were cruising the streets in the early hours, while fire roared through the arms factory. So he turned the bike towards home and ten minutes later they were dismounting with Coogan then pushing the BSA through the archway between the neighbouring house and along the short lane to his place behind the adjoining two-up two-down, Muffler behind.

He put the bike on its stand and looked up and at the sky, which had a huge red glow, flecked with arcing sparks and strands of smoke lit by the fire, he couldn't hear the crackling of it – the bells of fire engines dominated – but he could smell the burning. The streets, he had noticed as he piloted them back, were dotted with people gawping at the spectacle, when normally at this time they would be totally empty.

The house wasn't locked, he had little to steal, the furniture was scavenged and his battered old bakelite Bush radio wouldn't fetch a tanner for any thief. He put the kettle on, any action was therapeutic. Muffler had taken his scarf off. He looked to be about sixty, Coogan estimated, too old for military service.

'I don't know how you take it,' he said, 'You'll have to take it as it comes.'

Then, 'What do I call you?'

The man was rubbing his cold hands together. 'Better we don't exchange information, in case one or other is caught, then there's nothing to give away.'

Coogan nodded. The kettle was whistling, he scooped four teaspoons of tea into the teapot, and poured on the boiling water.

'If I had anything stronger I'd get it. My nerves are shot.'

'Call me Jim,' the other man said, 'that's as good a name as any.'

He paused. 'Unfortunately I know yours. I'm not boastful enough to think the bastards couldn't get it out of me under torture. Anyway, it won't take them long to make you the number one suspect. Then they'll be here. You need to get away.'

Coogan had found two cups from the sink which he quickly sluiced under the cold tap and now he was pouring the tea.

'There's no sugar or milk,' he said, handing over one of the cups, 'sorry…Jim.'

'Any idea where you'll go? I don't want to know where, just asking.'

'No, not really.' Coogan had a fanciful notion in his head. 'Liverpool and the boat to Ireland.' He shrugged. 'After that I don't know where. Just far.'

Jim, the other Jim, took a cautious sip of his tea. Both men were standing in the small kitchen that the outside door opened into.

'They won't be able to get you there, Ireland. You'll be safe.' He took another sip. 'No one to say goodbye to?'

Coogan shook his head. 'That's been done a while ago.' He took a big gulp of the tea, ignoring the pain in his throat.

'Have you got a pencil and some paper?' Jim asked.

'Somewhere. I'll look.' He put down the tea on the old table and opened the door to a small sideboard, pulling out a short pencil and an envelope. He took the letter from inside and handed the envelope and pencil over.

'Sorry, that's about all.'

Jim also put down his tea on he table and began scribbling on the back of the envelope.

'Here, that's one of our people in Liverpool. He may be able to help if you need it. Call him Archie. He's a small man with a bit of a limp, a memento of the first one. That's his address. Memorise it and then destroy this. If you say to him, "Can I interest you in health insurance?" He'll respond, "I've got my own thanks." He'll still be suspicious mind, you could be a plant, but the rest's up to you, to convince him. You're terrified look should do it.' Jim smiled briefly.

'Thanks.'

'Memorise and destroy. Remember. Thanks for the tea. I'm going. With luck we'll never see each other again. Or perhaps we can sup a beer and reminisce when this is all over, but I wouldn't count on it.'

He wound the scarf back round the lower part of his face, turned the door handle and slipped out. Before it closed behind him Coogan could still see the fiery glow in the sky.

He looked around the room, at the bare walls and the empty fireplace, he took the only ornament, a small black and white picture of a pretty girl in a gilt frame, and tucked it into one of the pockets of his leather jerkin. Then he went upstairs, took a change of clothing, underwear, shirt, jumper and socks from the low cupboard beside the unmade bed, went back downstairs and put the clothes on the table beside the two cups.

That was about it. Just the money he had managed to save, about twenty pounds, which he had hidden under a stretch of linoleum under the curtained, blackout window, which he pulled out and pocketed. He picked up his bundle, opened the door and went to the bike, stuffing everything into the saddle bag. He remembered the note on the table, he went back inside grabbed the envelope, memorised the address then took the matches from the fire surround and lit the envelope, leaving the ashes in the grate.

He hadn't quite told Jim the full truth about where he was going. Liverpool certainly, and Ireland, but from there he was going to try to get to France, somehow, and track down Fleur. He hadn't heard from her since she'd gone back, but he knew the town, her home town, which he hoped she could have gone back to. Or at least he might be able to find her relatives and see what they knew about where she was. It was crazy, he knew, putting himself back into the monster's mouth, but he had to trace her.

So, he told himself, you're going to go over to occupied France, without a word of German and just a few French phrases picked up from Fleur, none of them useful, somehow find her and be happy ever after. He shook his head over how ridiculous it was. If they catch you you'll be classed as a spy and shot. It's a suicide mission.

This time, for some reason, perhaps to convince himself he would be back, he locked the door and pocketed the keys.

2

June 1940, France

He hadn't had one of those falling dreams since he was a boy, it was splintered by flashing lights, what seemed like a crushing chest pain and that giddy emptiness and anxiety as he plunged downward out of control.

He woke slowly, his mouth thick, eyes failing to adjust, everything blurred, blinking, unable to focus. He started to gag, then tried to spit out what was clogging his mouth. His back prickled, he seemed to be naked and was clammy with cold sweat, and as he ran his right hand over his chest and stomach he felt a binding, coarse to the touch. He realised now that he was pulsing with pain, which seemed to sharpen his senses and bring everything into focus, the high wooden roof with crossed timbers with what seemed to be two pigeons looking down.

He tried to lift his head, only managing to get his chin to his chest. And then he noticed them. A young woman with a red bandana round her head, and a man, middle-aged, in sombre dark clothes. As he blinked and adjusted he saw that she was dressed in sloppy dungarees tucked into boots and was holding what looked like a shotgun down by her right leg. The man, with an angular, pinched face, red hair thinning and now, he saw, around his neck, the white spurt of a clerical collar.

'At last,' the man said. The priest. 'We were thinking it was never going to happen. It was very distracting.' He seemed to have a lilt in his voice.

He realised that he was lying on a bed of straw in what seemed to be a booth. An animal stall. Suppressing a yelp of pain he shuttled up onto his elbows. The girl was looking at him impassively, but it was the gun which centred his attention.

'Is this an execution?' he tried to make is sound light. 'Or a forced wedding?'

'Very good,' the priest said, 'you have a sense of humour. You'll need it. And a lot more.'

He seemed to nod to the girl, who was ignoring him. 'You'll be wanting to eat something I expect.'

It was an Irish accent, he caught it now. The priest was still looking to the girl, but she wasn't responding, still staring fixedly at him. He hoped she wasn't considering bringing the gun up.

'I'll be wanting to know where the fuck I am father, excuse my language. And her,' he motioned weakly with his head and, pain pumping through him, managed to get up into almost a sitting position. 'Is she dumb?'

The priest smiled. 'Dumb she surely isn't. She doesn't speak English. So I'm here to translate, and for the last rites if it had gone the other way.' He looked from her to him. 'And you should be nice to her, she saved your life.'

His memory was returning, in short bursts almost in time with his heartbeat, although it seemed to stop with him climbing through the entrails of an aeroplane. Before that just the jostle of bodies and noise, glimpses of squat buildings, leaden skies, flashing snaps of memory.

'Her name's Eugenie. You came down in her orchard. Into one of her apple trees. I'm afraid I can't tell you whether it was a Cox's Orange Pippin or a Bramley.' He smiled. 'Somehow she managed to cut you down, out of the parachute. That could be when you broke your ribs most likely. I'm sure she's sorry about that.'

She didn't seem to be regretting anything, just the same cold stare. She was pretty, he could see, from under the headscarf and through the smears of dirt on he face, high cheekbones, huge, dark eyes. He tried to smile at her but she didn't respond.

'She managed to drag you in here, cut the burned and torn uniform from you, washed you, smeared you with balm – or perhaps it was axle grease..? – covered you with straw and drove over to collect me. I don't think she wanted you in the house. Very wise. I'm Padraig Coyle, by the way. You? Couldn't tell from the dog tags.'

'Hmm?' He was still looking at her. It was coming back now, painfully, the strobing lights, the explosions, the rocking, bucking and yawing, the tearing sounds, the flames and then the endless fall.

'France,' he said, 'this must be France.'

'Certainement,' the priest replied. 'As I said, I'm here as the translator. Your spiritual adviser obviously, if called upon.'

'Merci,' he said to her. 'Merci beaucoup.'

It was about all the French he knew and it sounded stupid. She nodded her head slowly.

'Of course,' the priest was saying, 'in saving your life she's all but given up on hers. She should have handed you over to the Nazis. In fact that was one of the options I suggested but she rejected it out of hand. They'll shoot her if they discover you, if she's lucky and it's quick that is.'

'Merci,' he said again, now with more emphasis.

'Her name is Eugenie Silvestre. And you lad?'

'Robert Macaulay. Rab, or Mac, most people call me…what about,' he paused thinking of the consequences, '…what about the rest of my crew?'

He could see them all now. The skipper Roger Harrington, the toff they called him behind his back, Terry Small, the navigator, Jock Wilson the radio op, like him from Glasgow, Gerry Sullivan, incorrigible Gerry in the nose cone, his best mate Gary Pendleton, always with his arm round a different woman's waist, was, appropriately, the waist gunner…and him, the Tail End Charlie hunched over the four Brownings.

'Are they—?'

'I'm afraid that unless they're dangling fruit in another orchard it doesn't look good.' He nodded. 'I'll pray for them.'

He wanted to tell him to save his prayer, but he sank back onto the straw, the pain now secondary, he felt tears coming which he tried to cover up by passing his hands across his face and head. 'My hair?'

'We had to cut what was left of it off. Some of it was burned away. I expect it'll grow back. You've nasty burns on the back of your neck and lower down your back too. Genie put some cream on them. She swears it cures the cattle so you should be fine.'

'I need to get home,' he said staring up at the pigeons and the rafter. 'Back.'

'Not much chance of that lad,' Coyle was shaking his head. 'There's no way. The place is alive with Germans, the fighting is still going on but fortunately most of them are preoccupied with that. But we'll have to figure out what to do with you now. I told you what will happen to Genie if you're caught here. And the Huns aren't averse to shooting men of the cloth either. I don't think Ireland being out of the war would have much influence. Anyway,' he seemed to draw himself up to full height, a decision made, 'I've some brandy in the car which I'll fetch. Genie has made soup – I'm sure you're not picky, a vegetarian or something? It's in the kitchen. We'll get you up. I've brought you some clothes too, which may be a bit dull for your liking, priestly conservative, but that's it I'm afraid.'

'But no dog collar?' He tried to smile.

'No, no. Not even a tie. But perhaps Genie can fit you out better from her late dad's old stuff, although he was a bit smaller than you by the looks of it.'

He crunched back onto his elbows again into the straw.

'First the brandy,' he said.

They were hunched around an old and scarred table which seemed to have been cut from untrimmed oak, although as a city boy he wasn't sure that he had identified the wood correctly. Genie was sitting directly opposite him, still regarding him warily, but she had taken off the bandanna and her hair hung loosely around her shoulders, it was auburn with what seemed to be dots of red highlights. He was glad to see that the shotgun was propped against a corner wall. The priest, Coyle, was leaning back in his chair, puffing on a cigar, occasionally dropping ash into the unlit fireplace. A dog, he presumed a sheep dog, had appeared from somewhere and was lying under the table, he guessed at his mistress's feet. In front of them on the surface of the table, three chipped cups, full, almost to the brim, and the half-empty bottle of brandy.

He found it difficult to breathe, with the tight bandaging, and his back throbbed, but not so much now that the brandy had hit his empty stomach. His skin itched slightly too, the rough wool of the heavy jersey he supposed, his arms poked out of the sleeves which stopped several inches above his wrists, the trousers too, heavy, black, loose on him, stopped short of his bare ankles.

'It's difficult to say exactly what is happening. No doubt the Nazis and the BBC are both lying,' Coyle took another puff of his cigar and with his left hand deftly topped up his cup and the two others from the bottle then threw back a mouthful, rubbing his lips. 'What is pretty clear is that the attempt to get the armies off the shore at Dunkirk failed—-'

'We were trying to hit supply lines,' Mac came in.

'A few got away, we don't know how many, but the majority were caught, surrounded and bombarded and eventually surrendered.' Coyle shook his head, slowly. 'A tragic business.'

Mac took another sip of the rough brandy. 'I thought you were meant to be neutral fath- - Padraig?'

'There's no middle ground between good and evil lad, is there? We know what they've done, we've seen it in Belgium and Holland and here…no middle ground.'

Genie reached with her left hand and touched Coyle on the arm, then fired out what seemed like a list of questions, or demands, he couldn't understand. Coyle replied, rather more slowly, patted the girl's hand still with the cigar between his fingers.

'Well?' Mac asked.

'She wants me to tell you what happened with her father. He's a farmer, obviously…well he was. Two or three weeks ago, after the bulk of the Germans had passed through, fighting towards the coast, three soldiers, they may have been deserters, who knows, three men in uniform anyway, arrived and grabbed a pig from the yard….the only one they had left. A German detachment had already commandeered all the livestock. Well, commandeered isn't quite the right description. They shot most of the cattle and dragged the carcasses into trucks, presumably to help feed their men. Anyway Robert, her father, tried to stop them, one of them stabbed him with a bayonet. Genie saw this from the window and, this was the worst possible thing to do, ran out of the house to try to get to him. He was lying bleeding on the cobbles, trying to hold in his stomach when she reached him. They tore her off him and then they each raped her in the dirt while Robert bled out alongside her. She didn't want me to tell you that part, about the rapes.' He sighed. 'I pray he, Robert, wasn't conscious then.

He continued. 'She's not sure why they didn't kill her. She says they might as well have done. It could have been an armoured column arriving, or one of your Spitfires attacking it, whatever the reason all hell broke out and they ran away.

'She says her regret is that she didn't grab the shotgun when she first ran out, although obviously they would have shot her. And it,' he nodded towards the gun in the corner 'has never been far from her side since.'

Coyle shook his head slowly and fired the stub of the cigar into the fireplace.

'Jesus,' Mac said slowly.

'No, I'm afraid he wasn't there.'

'I'm so sorry,' he said, looking at her, not sure what else he could say. She seemed to nod her head, as if she understood. 'And her father, Robert?' he said now to the priest.

'I helped her bury him. We bundled him into a cart, wheeled him to the churchyard, we both took turns digging a grave. It was almost dark although the sky was lit by flashes of light, artillery, searchlights, it was so noisy I'm sure she couldn't hear my blessing. It wasn't possible to do it all properly.'

'So sorry,' he said again. Uselessly. 'And Genie?'

He was looking at her, she stared back, without a flicker of emotion on her face.

The priest shrugged. 'She'll never be the same again, obviously. She's a strong young woman. She'll rebuild, into what I don't know. But she will.'

Coyle grabbed his cup angrily and swallowed down the contents.

'She was having her period when they raped her, that's all that can be said for the good, that she won't be bringing an unwanted child into the world,' and he slammed the cup down on the table.

There was nothing to be said in the raging silence.

3

Forty-eight hours leave. Beck was looking forward to a hot bath, a change of clothes, more than a glass or two of fine wine – if there was one thing that this godforsaken country could do it was that! – and female company, whether offered or taken.

He had been billeted in what must have been a fine chateau before the war. Now there were tank tracks through the shrubbery, broken walls around a sunken garden with a large pond dry and full of leaves and mud. The house itself had taken a bruising, holes in the plasterwork where light and heavy fire had raked it and only two or three of the seventeen windows on the front fascia intact, the rest boarded up. All the effort had been put into cleaning up inside. Oriental carpets seemed untarnished by the conflict, draperies hung on the walls, the chandeliers cast a sparkling glow down to them, lighting up the portraits of the long-dead ancestors.

A massive lounge led to a wide, carpeted stairway, and his room, a suite really. He nodded to one or two of the uniformed men lounging on the settees and divans spread around, listening to what he thought must be something local coming from the gramophone, it was heavy on brass and strings, and made his way up the dark red route to his quarters. He had been assigned a trusted servant, someone called Albert, who spoke enough to be understood and who had, so he had been briefed, a comprehensive knowledge of what could be obtained. Probably a black marketeer, he thought.

When he opened the large double doors he could not have been more taken aback, although he didn't show it. A table, with white linen and polished cutlery, had been set in the middle of the room, a fire crackled in the grate, although it wasn't really a cold evening and, on the floor next to a dining chair, an ice bucket with the unmistakable top of a champagne bottle jutting out.

As he was staring at the table and then looking around, a door to his left opened, from a side room clearly, and a man who looked in his fifties, thick dark hair, with shuffling walk betraying a limp, came in. He had made an attempt to dress as a waiter, but it really hadn't worked. His black shirt was frayed at the collar, his trouser had been patched, Beck could see even from across the room – but he gamely had slung a white napkin across his left arm.

'You must be Albert?' he said, not waiting for a reply. 'My luggage, such as it is, is at the outside door. A tan leather suitcase and black holdall. Fetch it please and lay out my other uniform.'

Albert nodded and plucked the iced bottle from the bucket, quickly peeled the cork and popped it, turned upright a crystal glass and filled it, before handing it to Beck.

'I took the liberty of running a hot bath,' he said in halting German. 'I'll fetch your luggage and I'll serve dinner whenever you are ready. It isn't lavish—' he hesitated to find the right word, '– roast chicken with local paté, truffle, vegetables, there's a choice of wines, and then a cheese board and brandy.'

'Excellent. Certainly compared to the rations I've been used to lately,' Beck nodded. Certainly better than the men had been given, he thought, the men who had been stood down for just 24 hours and left to root for whatever they could find in twenty miles up to the line. He smiled, imagining the hunt for women in the vicinity. All the doors better be locked, not that that would stop them.

'I'll have that bath now,' looking to the door on his right, Albert nodding in confirmation, then picking up the glass of champagne and, almost as an afterthought, the ice bucket with bottle grumbling in the ice, and pushed through into the extravagantly tiled bathroom.

The bath had clearly been designed for more than one occupant, it stood like a wide petal on brass feet in the centre of the room, steam wisping from it. Hot water, he thought, what a luxury, how on earth do they manage it? Coal, wood from around here to fire the boiler – he had noticed that the town was almost surrounded by forests – so fuel would not be a problem. Slowly he peeled off his soiled uniform and climbed into the scented water.

He lost count of how long he was soaking in the water, until it became tepid and the champagne was finished. Albert had knocked, brought in clean underwear and his sponged and ironed second uniform and laid it carefully over a chair. Now he was sitting at the dining table, the piled plate slid onto the damask mat in front of him.

'Albert,' he said after the first mouthful, 'this is delicious. They say that you're a man who knows everything and everyone around here, is that the case.'

'Perhaps a slight exaggeration, sir.'

'You limp a bit. Did you get that in the first one?'

'At Mons. A piece of your shrapnel.'

Beck put down fork and chuckled. 'No hard feelings I take it?'

'It was a long time ago, sir.'

'And what did you do before this one?'

'I had a small grocer's shop…well, the only one.'

When he looked closer at the man Beck picked out keen blue eyes, a narrow nose which had been broken at some point, and high cheekbones. He was a lean man indeed.

'So you know just about everybody and how to get things?'

'Within reason of course.'

'Company,' Beck continued, 'any ideas Albert?'

'Female sir?'

Beck laughed. 'Oh indeed. Female, young, pretty or what passes for it, someone who would keep a German officer happy for a few hours.'

He could see that the older man was shifting uncomfortably on the spot, not looking at him.

'Ah, so you do know someone Albert? Someone comely who would like to be entertained, rewarded even, as you would be?'

Beck knew that he would give up a name. Lord knows how people are eating with the war exploding around them, he thought. Everything edible had been taken, consumed, animals slaughtered and barbecued, shops raided. God, they were even eating the fallen horses.

'I will be absolutely discreet,' he said into the silence.

'I do know of someone. A very nice girl, young, very pretty. And healthy, if you understand me?' Beck nodded. 'I could enquire?'

'Deutschmarks for you and her.' Beck said, taking a bite of the moist chicken and pouring a glass of what the label said was Sancerre – a new one on him – into his glass. 'A deal?'

'Leave it with me,' Albert responded and shuffled from the room.

The haupsturmführer brushed at the collar and shoulders of his black uniform to clear any specks of dandruff or hairs that might be there. Alfred had done a nice job, he thought as he walked into the market square, now empty, most of the shops blackened and with their fronts blown out. There was what passed for a bar, still with dark blackout curtains, through which a sliver of light escaped. He wandered if the girl was known there.

He had her description, quite tall, slim, she'd be wearing a loose coat (which concealed her wonderful figure, Albert had promised) and a beret tilted at an angle. She'd be carrying a hymn sheet, which seemed odd. Perhaps there was a shortage of newsprint? She had to be discreet, he understood that, the locals wouldn't take kindly to fraternisation, and she also had to avoid the patrols and the curfew. She was taking a big risk, he understood that too. Still, she'd have her reward. He smiled.

He passed an army patrol, two lounging men, who immediately snapped to attention when they noticed the SS uniform as he came up to them. Bareheaded, he nodded to them and walked on. The rendezvous was at a statue, a memorial to someone, or perhaps to many, who had died in the Great War. There were no street lights, although the risk of an RAF attack was minimal. But there was a hazy half moon which yellowed the paving stones as he picked his way, as Albert's instructions, to the spot.

It was a night to enjoy, the war was all but over, but for the final attack on Britain, he was refreshed, just the right amount of alcohol to make him almost carefree. And still a day of his leave to come. The girl, he thought, as he came up to the memorial, if she wasn't all that was promised, he'd dismiss her with a few marks, or perhaps just turn her back, bend her over and get on with it.

He heard the drone of planes above, he recognised the engine sounds, ours he thought, on their way to dump on what remained of the English. He had reached the square now. He struck a match, not so much to illuminate, but let anyone, or rather her, know that he was here. There was a sound to his left, he wheeled round, but it was only a scurrying cat, one of the few which hadn't yet been eaten.

The square and the statue were on the lip of the forest which reared black against the grey sky. He could make out a path and then a figure hurrying towards him. It was her, Laure, that was the name he had been given, and when she came close to him, her coat open and ruffling as she walked, he saw that he wouldn't be disappointed, that she was more than pretty.

She took his hand. 'Quick,' she said in German, 'before we're spotted' and she pulled him back onto the forest path, stopping briefly to give him a quick peck on the cheek, before guiding him further in.

They must have walked about a hundred metres, saying nothing, when she nudged him through a clump of small bushes into a clearing, pine husks chattering as they stumbled in. It was dark but her face seemed almost ghostly to him. She was wearing lipstick, he could taste it as she kissed him now, guiding him gently forward and so that she stopped with her back to a tree, him in front of her. She smelled of scent, he couldn't tell what it was, something cheap probably, but it didn't matter, his hands were inside her coat rubbing on her breasts, biting gently on her lower lip, and now he felt her hand rub on his groin, encouraging his erection, then both hands scrabbling for his belt buckle.

His head was snapped back, something had grabbed onto his hair, his legs were kicked behind the kneecaps, bringing him onto his knees, he briefly saw the glint of the knife blade before it cut through his exposed neck in a burst of blood.

'Watch the blood on his uniform, we'll need it,' Laure said.

Haupsturmführer Werner Beck did not hear her.

4

'Are you a Catholic son?'

'Why Padraig, do you want to hear my confession?'

Coyle smiled. 'Not now.'

He was backlit by the glow from the last of the day's sun, refracted through a kitchen window. It gave him an aura, Mac thought, appropriate for a priest. The barrels of Genie's shotgun seemed to sparkle as the light hit them.

'She isn't in the room, and she's left the gun, so does that mean she trusts me?' Mac wondered out loud.

Coyle chuckled. 'No, because she's unloaded it and taken the cartridges with her. And she probably reckons she could outrun you, the state you're in. Or knock you down with the stock.'

'I hope she will,' Mac said quietly. 'Trust me I mean. In time, if I have any….and no Padraig I'm not. A Catholic. I don't have religion. My parents were. But that's another life.'

He had lost track of time. It was now almost two days since he had surfaced again, four or five days since they had taken off from Manston. He had spend hours since on alert, waiting for German soldiers to arrive. It could only be a matter of time. Peering from the kitchen at the road at the bottom of the field in front of the house, scanning with binoculars he supposed were Genie's father's. They were well used, in a battered brown leather case, the smell of which reminded him of the belt his stepfather had used on him. There had been a lot of traffic along the road, heavy army lorries, tanks on low loaders, towed artillery pieces, the constant drone of war.

Coyle got up from his chair, briefly left the room, and came back with a small brown case, which he held out. 'You'll need to change.'

Mac took it. 'I don't understand,' he said, flicking open one of the two catches.

'When I asked you whether you were a Catholic or not I wasn't trying to add you to my flock. Look inside, you'll understand.'

Mac swung the case onto the kitchen table, and freed the other catch. A clerical collar on a background of black looked up at him.

He dropped the lid of the case back down. 'What is this?' He asked.

'We have an appointment, at the church. It's just in case we get stopped on the way. You're my new assistant, Father Dermot O'Malley, just arrived from Ireland a few days ago. You don't speak French or German. Just keep you mouth shut and smile. Hopefully that will do it.' He didn't add, but I doubt it.

Mac opened the lid of the case again and took out the stiff white collar, thinking that this wasn't much of a plan.

He sat with his head down, a bible in his hand, mumbling occasionally, as if he were praying. The starched collar rubbed his Adam's Apple. Occasionally he put a finger under it to loosen it. The heavy clothes, the dark serge jacket felt unwieldy, as if it didn't belong to him. He smiled briefly, because obviously it didn't. He was aware that people were coming and going behind him, the rustling of clothing, the clack of heels on the flagstones, men mainly, he could make that out when he darted his head to the side briefly, making their way to the confessional and then leaving. The other sound was the faint hum of voices coming from the booth, although he could not make out the words. Besides, they'd be in French so no point even trying to listen.

After more than an hour, when he was dozing, there was a loud cough behind him and he turned to see Coyle looking down at him, the stole round his neck dangling as he leaned forward.

'Purple doesn't suit you Father,' he said. 'It clashes with the hair.'

'Follow me my son,' the priest said, nodding is head towards the altar and walking away. Mac put the bible down on the pew beside him and followed him, their footsteps pattering softly on the cold floor, through a heavy oak door, down a dark corridor and into a small, windowless room, the only light coming from a small lamp on a table covered in a white cloth. As he looked around he could just make out a wardrobe and sideboard and two cane chairs set beside the table.

'Sit,' the priest said in a low voice, then turned and locked the door behind him, before taking off the purple stole, folding it and laying it on the table, and sitting down on the vacant chair.

Once more Mac wondered why Coyle was putting himself at such risk for him.

'Well,' Coyle said eventually, as if he had read his thoughts, 'it seems the Germans are getting organised. They're going to requisition houses and billet officers with local people. This will begin to happen tomorrow, or even tonight, so it won't be safe at Genie's —-'

'She won't be safe,' he broke in, 'after what's happened to her.'

'She has relatives in town here. She doesn't get on with them and she's saying she won't go. I'll make sure she moves out if it happens.'

Mac nodded. 'I have to get out of here,' he said, 'and home.'

The priest shook his head. 'That can't be done right now. There's too much chaos for the time being.'

'Surely that should be the right time, while there's turmoil?'

He stood up impatiently, the sharp spurt of pain in his ribs chastising him.

'Sit down son' the priest said. 'The truth is, apart from anything else, we don't have the means of getting you away.'

'We?' He asked.

'Ok, the resistance, Maquis, such as it is. We…they, can't risk people. There are more important matters to deal with. And you can help.'

Mac nodded. 'I owe you. And Genie.'

'Good lad,' the priest slapped him lightly on the shoulder. 'Things are very bad. There was an attempt to take your regiments off the beaches at Dunkirk, but it failed. Heavy seas and German bombardment. We're hearing that not many got away.'

Mac let it sink in.

'We were trying to hit their supply columns,' he replied. 'Then the plane was hit, I remember that now, ground fire I think, because I didn't see any Messerschmitts, although the air was thick with them over the Channel. There was our Wellington and seven others. Three Hurricanes with us part of the way…I saw one go down. But I hadn't even opened fire on anything. And then the rest is pretty hazy. Until…' he thought of the crew, his chums, and prayed to himself that at least some of them had got out of the plane and he wasn't the sole survivor.

'How many missions did you carry out?'

'Hmm? That was the eighteenth. About double the average so I guess I was due it.'

'I'm sorry Mac,' the priest put his hand on the shoulder briefly again before taking it away. 'From what we hear there's been a surrender by your navy. At least by the fleet supposedly guarding the Channel and the southern approach. And there's been some kind of political coup, Churchill's either dead or has fled—'

'How do you know all this Padraig?'

He smiled. His face looked almost jaundiced in the muted light from the lamp.

'The confessional isn't just for hearing sins. It's where you can unburden yourself, tell your spiritual father all that's going on. Just because the French army has been broken, destroyed, doesn't mean the people have been, it doesn't mean that they'll meekly accept the Nazis' commands. And they have ears and eyes and can report what they've seen. The Germans need our people to service them, work for them, and from small threads you can build up a tapestry of information.'

'Very poetic, Father,' Mac said dryly.

'It's one of my favourites,' the priest responded. 'And we have radios. Not just your Home Service,' he smiled again. 'We have communications expertise you know, we're not all dumb peasants —'

'And men of the cloth.'

'Yes indeed. But it's not looking good at all. There's talk of a German expeditionary force setting out for Britain, across the Channel. If not now, I suppose soon. Here they're rounding up tens of thousands of soldiers, British and French, and they have their hands full and dealing with it. We'll have to add to their problem.'

'Padraig,' Mac cut in, 'you are a very unusual priest.'

'I like to think so,' the older man replied quietly. 'I was never sold on the cheek turning example.'

'You have a plan?'

'Not quite, but there is one germinating.'

There was silence for several breaths.

'But there must be others here, in the town, who have eyes and ears for the Germans? Traitors.'

The priest nodded. 'Indeed. We've got a pretty good idea who they are. The ones who have been vocal before the war and into it, the ones calling for peace, rather than surrender, which is the same thing. The Third Republic is over I'm afraid and there will be collaborators. No doubt about that. Most people I suppose will just want to get on with whatever is left of their lives, trying to get by, some will see the personal and profitable advantages of grabbing the Deutschmark. But there will be resisters. They may be too old for military service, disabled or too young for it, but they'll be our secret army, the Ceux de la Résistance.'

'And women?'

Mac thought of Genie and what she had gone through, the shotgun which did not leave her side.

'Women are crucial,' the priest agreed. 'Absolutely vital.'

He reached over, pulled up the damask cloth on the table, reached under and pulled out a box. 'You sure you won't have a cigar?' He opened the box lid and held it out.

'No thank you.'

'Oh well,' the priest sighed, 'I might as well.'

He lifted the box lid, dug out a cigar, put the box back on the table, thrust his right hand into a jacket pocket, rummaged in it and pulled out matches and a small silver cigar cutter, lopped the end of the cigar and lit it.

'I almost forgot,' he leaned forward, smoke curling up from the cigar in his right hand, and thrust his left hand once more under the cloth. 'This is for you.'

Sitting up he handed what looked like an ancient revolver to Mac. 'It might not look the part, it's what they call a Lebel, from the first war. Eminently reliable. Takes 8mm ammunition. It's loaded and I can get you a couple of boxes of ammo. You never know, you might need it.'

Mac held it in his right hand. It looked in good condition, it was well greased, he fumbled for a couple of seconds before he found the catch which snapped open the chamber.

'It's a bit different to the Webley,' he said, 'But pretty sensible and it looks like it'd be quicker to load I think, it doesn't have to be broken open.'

'Get used to it,' Padraig told him, 'And keep it with you.' He drew on the cigar. 'Now, we have to find you a safe place to stay. And I think I have just that place.'

5

The house had been in the family for three generations, standing on the brow of the hill which gave a view down to the town below, backing onto a small field and then the dense woodland which ran up to the first slopes of the mountains. It was modelled on the French baroque style, the rough blocks cut from limestone in the quarry two miles away and transported by horse and cart and muscle to the site. Stone that came free because the Dubois family owned the quarry. The house had twelve bedrooms, although now only one was in regular use, all of the rooms had had elaborately corniced ceilings, some of them now chipped, and it cost the very devil to heat, which was why the radiators were turned off in the unused rooms.

It wasn't that he couldn't afford to heat them, there was just no point. Downstairs was warm, the lounge now had a roaring log fire that Marta, the housekeeper, regularly topped up, although he really should do more to help her as she was well into her sixties now. He chuckled, looking around the room, with the chandeliers sparkling above, the faces of his ancestors and their hobbies – horses and foxes predominated – in pictures on the wall. He took it all in and he felt proud of himself.

He was holding a filled champagne flute in his hand, the silver bucket holding the bottle, on the carved table next to the sofa, was drizzling condensation and he was sure he could hear the ice crackling. Or perhaps that was the fire?

He was standing at a window watching the small convoy of vehicles disappear through the large gates at the bottom of the drive as the day, a very, very exciting and rewarding day, began to fade.

Paul Dubois had no children at home. The truth was that when they had left for university, they had left him and his wife, Sophie. She left what seemed like minutes later, although it had been a week or two, perhaps more. There couldn't be a divorce, of course, and he had ensured that she would get nothing from him, alive or dead. That probably played a part in his ostracisation by the three girls, the young Sophie, Angelique and Laure. They didn't write or call and he didn't keep in touch. Two of them had married, Sophie and Laure, and there were grandchildren, five he was sure, but he had never seen them. If it was a loss, as outsiders might think, then he was bearing it well, he thought, although I must avoid being smug.

The taillights had disappeared now. He took a sip of champagne and turned away from the window. Marta had left for the day, his cold supper was set out in the kitchen, with a bottle of crisp white wine waiting for him. In a little while. He put down his glass next to the sweating ice bucket and switched on the gramophone. He didn't know much about classical music, his taste didn't extend far beyond Beethoven, he selected his Fifth from the rack of albums, gingerly pulled the disc from its sleeve and dropped it onto the turntable and pulled over the arm of the player and let it fall on the record. Music

47

began to fill the room, he sat down on one of the leather armchairs and stared into the fire. It had been a fine day indeed.

The German commandant, Kreisler, he had his card somewhere, had been very polite and meticulous. He had worn those military jodhpurs and high boots, glazed to a shine, which he didn't heel click, which was a shame. His adjutant, he forgot the name, or hadn't listened attentively enough to register, had stood a couple of paces behind the chair in which Kreisler sat down. The chap didn't look much older than a teenager, but perhaps this was just a symptom of him growing older. The boy/man had a vivid duelling scar down his left cheek. He hadn't said a word, just the occasional nod, as the superior officer spoke. There were ten or twelve soldiers too, but they stood outside, guarding their master he supposed.

Kreisler spoke excellent French, which was probably why he was picked for the job, and he wasted no time in coming to the point.

'Monsieur Dubois, I am here to ask for your co-operation. The war is over as far as France is concerned and soon it will be over with England too and we can return to calm and order. The Führer has no wish to punish the French people, just those who aided your government in this war. So I am here as, let's just say, an emissary.'

Kreisler paused, waiting for a response, but Dubois merely smiled. 'We wish to mitigate the suffering of your people…I say your people because I'm told you are leader here.'

Dubois nodded his head and held his palms out in a gesture of supplication. 'My family has been here for a very long time.'

The German, who had a clipped moustache and, Dubois thought, looked too old to be a soldier, nodded. 'We have done our research and we know that you were very much opposed to your country declaring war against mine.'

He was waiting for confirmation Dubois thought, so he nodded his head slowly. Kreisler, he thought must be in his mid-fifties, hair also in a bristle cut, hooded blue eyes, an air of complete self-assurance, someone who must be used to unquestioning obedience.

He felt he was obliged to say something in response.

'No one wants any more suffering. Of course. People have been through enough, more than enough. Many of the people here work for me, in the quarry or the farm or the slaughterhouse. I feel my responsibility to them heavily.'

He knew that it sounded pompous but, why be modest, it was true.

'Good,' Kreisler smiled and crossed his leg. Dubois could see the reflection from the chandelier above dancing on the instep of his right boot. 'That is just what I wanted to hear. We would like you to use your influence here to reassure not just your workers, but the townspeople, that we can be the benevolent power, unless, of course...' he left the threat unsaid.

'There is much to be done,' he continued. 'I don't have the time or the inclination to be involved in the day-to-day of this area, to oversee. We're still at war of course, although not for long. I'm asking you to assume that mantle, to become the leader, the mayor, whatever title fits, you can recruit a panel of similarly-thinking people if you need them and be, not responsible to me, but be my partner. In a joint venture for peace and prosperity.' He paused. 'There will be rewards.'

'Well,' Dubois replied, gauging how far he could go, 'I am very busy. I have my businesses to run you know.'

Kreisler uncrossed his legs and leaned forward, his adjutant seeming to shiver with tension. 'Of course. I completely understand. But I could simplify it. So that you didn't have to go through that tedious business of markets, subject to flows, ups and downs, and all of the costs of doing it. I can guarantee to take all of your produce, vegetables, meat, fruit, even wine, at a margin above market price. Say 25 per cent? And I'm sure our armies will need stone and sand and grit too.'

Dupont didn't need to long to think about it. Not just my produce, he thought, I can buy in the market and supply the Nazis and pocket the mark up.

'That, Herr Kreisler, is a very attractive proposition.'

'We have a deal?' Kreisler standing up and holding out his hand.

'I'll get started on forming a cabinet in the morning.' Dubois couldn't help but grin as he took the German commander's hand.

He didn't realise that he must have nodded off. It was the clicking of the gramophone arm at the end of the record that woke him. He got up, shook his head to remove the muzziness, walked over to the teak cabinet and switched off.

But the noise had not stopped.

It took him a few seconds but he could begin to identify the sounds. They were coming from outside, gravel crunching, muttered voices. It was now as dark as it was going to get. Through the window he could see the last embers of sundown. He couldn't remember ordering anything, there was no reason why anyone should be outside now. If it was one of the workers from the farm there would be trouble. He felt his anger rise, then poured himself a small measure of the almost flat champagne, threw it back, and walked to the door feeling the spring of the Turkish carpet underneath his feet.

The door was unlocked, he felt sure he had locked it after Marta left, he rotated the brass knob and pulled open the heavy wooden door.

There seemed to be three of them, in the dusk he couldn't make out faces, just indistinct shapes, two bent over, huddling against the wall, hats pulled down and scarfs around their mouths, the third just standing looking at him. Unmasked, a vaguely familiar face.

'What are you doing here?' he said, voice raised, glancing away to the two who had stopped and straightened up. He realised they had paint brushes in their hands. 'Who are you?'

He looked back at the one in front of him, in a trench coat, beret pulled down almost to the eyebrows, the ruby sky behind him as the day went.

'You are a collaborator and traitor to France,' he heard.

It was the third one, the one without the mask.

'Don't be ridiculous—'

Now he saw that the figure's right arm was extended towards him.

The first bullet hit him in the stomach, knocking him back and as his legs collapsed he fell back on the gravel, the pain raging though him, everything in his body seeming to arc and overload, his face looking up at the streaked sky, the colour bleeding out of it. Then the shape of the person over him, the hole in the muzzle aimed at his nose.

'I know who you are, you—' he said. The blast of the gun cut off the rest of the sentence.

'It's done.'

One of the others said. 'It's time to go.'

Drips ran from the word splattered in red paint on the limestone wall. *Collaborateur.* Slowly leaking down the stone as the last of Dubois blood stained the grey gravel.

6

The Eglise Saint-Jean sat on a barren, rocky hill above the town, on the highest point before the mountains behind, as if it gave God a better overview of what was going on below. There was no record of who built it, which was surprising, although it was said that it had originally been constructed some time in the 12th century. It's internal walls, if you looked closely enough, were pitted by tiny scratched engravings, crosses etched into the hard stone, left by soldiers off to a crusade. If it was scored through it meant that the one who had done it had come back, at least alive. Most of the crosses had not been cancelled. There are similar graffiti in the Church of the Holy Sepulchre in Jerusalem, perhaps carved by the same ones as here.

It was almost a mile from the village, along a stony track which took a series of zigzags before it reached the gates, and from there it was an even steeper haul to the doors of the church and the hall and small house behind. Which made carrying a coffin from home to the final destination a muscular task. On Sundays the elderly, the hobbling women, the stumbling men in their shiny best suits, took an age to climb the gradient, but they did, unless they were bed bound, and even then relatives might pull them in wheelchair or, and it was not too uncommon, by a horse or donkey. If they were wealthy enough, and there were few of those, they came in well polished but aged cars, which they parked outside the church gates on a small plateau which had been chiselled out of the hill.

That was the village approach. To the left as you looked at it the land fell away into scree and boulders, where only mountain goats could traverse, and on the other side thick razor-edged gorse. Behind the church and to the right still as you faced it, a graveyard the size of two football fields, on another unnatural-seeming plateau which had been levelled and built up by generations before, hewing rock and carrying away the stones which had been used to build the rough wall which arced round the church grounds, or at least three-quarters of the way, when they had either run out of rock or resilience.

The graveyard had been created for the wealthy of the area and so it was largely covered with elaborate, iron and steel and slate mausoleums, the majority of which were built in the 18th and 19th century, baroque and gothic architecture, sometimes a mix of both. Or none, just plain and stern. They had been put up by successors to honour their ancestors, or more likely as a show of wealth and status. At the back of the graveyard a wicker gate led to a narrow path on a descending ridge which fed into the engulfing forest and mountains beyond, the track growing more sparse and difficult to follow as it wound through the trees and up to the stone peaks, which looked so close you could touch them, or drive a piton into them, although they were the best part of a mile away.

'This place is meant to be haunted,' Coyle said. 'Some of the locals…most of them, believe that. They wouldn't come up here after dark.'

They had come out of the back door of the church and were looking across the grave furniture, the zinc crosses, the statues and small columns, to the trees and slopes beyond.

'I've never been able to establish if it's one ghost or if there's a whole haunting party of them.' He smiled and nudged Mac, who winced. 'I've been disappointed, I haven't seen one yet.'

'Perhaps it's the white collar or the cross round your neck that puts them off? Or your flaming red hair dancing out of your skull like the the fires of hell?'

Coyle looked at him. 'You're feeling better then?'

'That jab in the ribs didn't hasten recovery Padraig,'

'I forgot,' the priest said. 'I'm sorry.'

They stood for a moment, the sun high above, the sky mottled here and there by small puffs of cloud. It reminded Mac of the bursts of anti-aircraft fire on missions and that sent a wave of sadness through him. Or was it survivor guilt? Had any of the others got out? It didn't seem likely.

'Why are we standing here? What is it you want to show me?'

'It's your new lodgings. Or at least an emergency bolthole. Come this way.'

He put his hand on Mac's elbow and tugged him gently and along the pebbled path between the graves and the mausoleums. Half way along they took a left onto another path where weeds were springing up between the stones and after a few steps the priest halted. He nodded his head towards a small, stained marble building, about two metres high to the peak of the flat roof, slightly wider than that, two columns framing each side of a battered metal door.

'You're not serious?'

He was trying to read in the priest's face whether this was a joke

'It's only temporary. And in an emergency. It's empty, has been for over a hundred years since some relatives of the deceased took the coffin and buried it somewhere else. I don't think they were body snatchers, it was some dispute between two branches of the family and the coffin was removed a year or two after his death. The man buried here was called Pierre Lefevre – you can just about make out the name carved above the door – who was a local landowner and early industrialist. He had a factory, somewhere outside Paris, an iron works making rails for railways I think. He may have made some of the early ones for the Brest to Paris line, but I'm probably just making that up. His family came from here and he bought a small farmhouse a couple of miles from here and retired early. He was killed, ironically, on the railway line. Most people thought it was suicide, but somehow the priest here at the time was persuaded it wasn't, probably through a large donation, so he could be buried on consecrated ground.'

Mac stared at the battered, building.

'There couldn't have been much left to bury.'

Coyle chuckled. 'No, they could probably carry away the coffin underarm...But anyway, it's empty, there's a deep crypt, about eight feet so it is, with steps down to it. And I have a key. I've checked it out. And I've swept it out. It's cold, I won't pretend otherwise, but, as I said, it's only for emergencies, and until we can work out a way to get you home when this all dies down.'

He paused in thought for a few seconds. 'When it does it will became even more dangerous as the Huns get organised and there's more presence.'

Mac looked at the building and felt a shiver on his spine.

'Is there any update on what's happening? Any word from Britain?'

'Not a lot and none of its good. Apparently Churchill is dead, the Nazis are in Westminster, a task force has taken a bite out of the south of England, an occupation, but most of the rest of the country seems unoccupied. It'll just be a matter of time before the rest is, I suppose.' He sighed. 'I know we're neutral in this but I really don't understand what my government is doing. You can't be neutral to fascism.' He shook his head. 'Don't get me started on Irish history and politics.'

Coyle rummaged in the right-hand pocket of his jacket and pulled out a large and heavy key. 'Let's take a look.' And they both walked across the neatly-cut grass to the door of the mausoleum.

7

August 1940

'Am I a prisoner, young man?'

'No Prime minister, of course you're not. It's for you own safety sir.'

Churchill could see that the young marine, well he presumed he was a marine although he was in civilian dress, was embarrassed and unsure of what to do. He tried to smile reassuringly, but it came across as a tight grimace.

'Then there's nothing to prevent me getting into this cage and going to the surface?'

Not that he knew how to work the damn thing.

'No sir. It would probably get me demoted, or worse, but no sir, nothing.'

'What is your name young man?'

'It's Griffiths sir. James.'

'And what age are you Griffiths James.'

'Twenty-one sir.'

'I see you've learned how to use emotional blackmail early Griffiths.'

Churchill had put on a heavy, dark serge overcoat over his flying suit and was holding a black homburg hat in his right hand, with difficulty, given the large cigar that was between his first and second fingers. In his left hand he held a wad of papers.

'I didn't mean——'

'Shush lad, I was only teasing.'

He looked around at the cavern walls. 'I never realised how much I would miss the open air. I saw a lot of it as a young man, all over the world, most of it under shot and shell, or about to receive a dose of it. And now I see it in my dreams. Bright, blue English skies without a Messerschmitt or a bloody Heinkel blotting it.'

He raised his right arm with the hat and Cuban cigar, plopped the hat on his head, freeing him to tap Griffiths on the shoulder. The young sergeant caught a whiff of the dry musk of tobacco.

'Of course I don't want you to be cashiered. So get your superior officer and tell him that I have ordered you to take me to the surface. I'll wait here. I promise you.'

'Very well sir.'

Griffiths gave a quick salute, more a touch to his forehead, did a sharp about turn and left almost in a run, the Enfield rifle in his left hand at waist level. Churchill watched him scurry away into the lighted tunnel, his steps crackling on the sand and fragments of coal. He knew that the soldiers' mess was about twenty yards along the cavern, he had heard the sounds coming from it days before and walked along to find where the noise was coming from. There was a narrow opening, a cardboard sign nailed above it, 'All welcome' scrawled on it – so there was no division between officers and men, he noted – and when he looked into the hollowed out space, battened like everywhere, there were three or four tables inside, upturned ammunition crates for seats, and in the harsh flickering light he saw that three men were playing cards, tin mugs on the table between them.

He stepped in. 'It says all are welcome, so that presumably includes me?' he had said.

It took the men a couple of seconds to realise who the visitor was and then, almost as if on command, they dropped their cards on the table and snapped to attention, one of the cases clattering over.

'At ease chaps,' he had said. 'I don't wish to disturb you. I was just exploring. As you were, or whatever the command is you military lads respond to.'

But he could see that they were embarrassed and unsure what to do, so he had said, 'On you go. I'll get back to my quarters,' and he had left.

Now, standing next to the wire cage, he could hear raised voices coming along the hewn corridor although he couldn't make out what was being said, then the tramp of feet and a tall man he knew as Captain Rogers, a Cambridge man he had learned from another officer, a rugger blue and another in, was it something in athletics? And as he got closer, Griffiths behind, Churchill could see that he was barely containing his rage

'Rogers,' Churchill said, getting in first, 'you mustn't blame the lad. I told him I am going up.'

'You can't Prime Minister,' the captain spat out, 'I —-'

'Can't captain?' Churchill butted his head towards the man. 'You are presuming to tell me what I can and can't do!'

'No sir. Sorry, I didn't mean it that way.' Rogers, like all the other soldiers, was in civvies. Looking at his suit Churchill reckoned these were Savile Row civvies. 'It's just—'

Churchill cut him off with a wave of his cigar. 'I've made a decision and, as you may have gathered, I'm not one to go back on it. Griffiths here will accompany me. We'll be like moles in the night, coming up for air.' And he punched Rogers lightly in the chest with the hand holding the cigar.

The man took a deep breath. 'Can I just point out Prime Minister that you'd be endangering not just your own life, but every man here sir.'

Churchill laughed and turned to glance at the younger man. 'I see where you learned the emotional blackmail Griffiths. It's about the first thing you're taught at public school, eh Rogers, although buggery may come before. What do you say?'

'I don't…I don't know what to say sir, just that it's reckless. And dangerous.'

He had thin face and a narrow mouth below an extravagant moustache, long sideburns. Churchill could see that at his waistband under the open jacket he was carrying a holstered pistol.

'I'm 65 years old Rogers, what age are you, 28, 29?

'Thirty-two sir.'

'Well I've seen a bit of danger in my 65 years and I've been reckless too. And I would not do anything to endanger the men here. But I've been down here so long that even you are beginning to look attractive to me….Don't look so shocked man that was a joke. I won't take any risks, we'll keep in cover and Griffiths here will guard me and advise me. I just need to smell fresh air, not the damp recycled stuff here, and see the sky. I do have a soul under this battered and somewhat corpulent exterior…Smile man.'

Rogers seemed to give it a moment's thought, although he really had no choice.

'Very well Prime Minister, I can't restrain you. But any consequences will be your responsibility.'

'Yes, yes man. As always' Churchill replied, turning to the lift cage. 'Now how the devil do you operate the damn thing?'

Rogers had somehow warned men on the surface, probably by intercom, that they were on their way from the deep because two figures in miner's clothes, hard hats but helmet lights not lit, were waiting as they opened the cage and stepped out. The two had attempted to smear their faces with coal dust but it was apparent from their bearing and size that this was disguise – miners, Churchill had observed, were on the dwarfish side, which was probably a necessary attribute, or lack of it, when crawling along a narrow seam with a pickaxe – and that they were soldiers.

'Gentlemen,' he greeted them, touching the brim of his homburg as he stepped out of the cage in front of Griffiths. 'Thankfully that damn thing comes up a lot slower than it goes down.'

'Sir,' the even taller one whispered. 'Please just sit where we put you. We have excellent lookouts and security and you'll be isolated from most of the mine activity. We're driving some trucks in as kind of barrier, we'll have a cover story, doing some maintenance on this old shaft, to prevent collapse, or pumping out water. So as long as you don't move about it should be fine.'

'Show me to my appointed place. Which is a phrase I very seldom use.'

Now he and his young minder, Griffiths had left his weapon below, were sitting together on a bench which had been dragged out of a shed, with a view through the gap between two other buildings to the high perimeter fencing and, far in the distance, the dark hills, which looked pasted onto the grey sky. There was a half moon above, a milky, ghoulish light on them and the stars were pinpricks.

'Bullet holes' Churchill said out loud. 'I suppose that's what this bloody business has driven me to, every thought is about war,' puffing on his cigar.

'If you don't mind me asking, sir,' Griffiths said, shuffling on the bench, 'where do you get them from, they're huge cigars?'

Churchill tapped his nose, with the hand holding the cigar. 'Actually from our good friends in Cuba. They were about the only thing I grabbed when I had to make my hasty retreat from Downing Street. Not even my paints and canvases.'

'What about your wife sir?'

'Mmhm? Clemmie's on her way to the United States, may even have got there by now.' He blew a cloud of smoke into the air. 'What about you Griffiths, were you one of the few who came back from France?'

'No sir, I was just coming to the end of my training. Another fortnight and I'd have been on my way.'

'Well at least you were saved from that. We tried but...' Churchill's words trailed off. 'So you've seen no action.'

'Apart from a few shots at the Huns on the outskirts of London before were ordered to retreat, no.'

Churchill slapped the young soldier lightly on the knee. 'Don't worry, my boy. You are going to have plenty of opportunity.'

They sat for a time, each contemplating their past, recalling what they had lost, until Churchill, looking up at the sky, said, 'Are they ours or theirs? My eyesight isn't what it was.'

Griffiths looked up at what seemed a swarm of dots inching across the bright moon. 'Theirs, sir. They'll be off to bomb around Birmingham or further north probably. The RAF boys will catch them if they do, I pray.'

Churchill tapped the folder beside him on the bench. 'Now that the Bosche have all our southern airfields they can cover almost the whole country. From the north of France too. I've given instructions not to engage them until they're somewhere north of Oxford. We wouldn't want a dog fight over our ancient spires, would we?....In truth it wouldn't bother me in the slightest if they obliterated the place, as long as there was no loss of life...there are too many of their graduates in the civil service, the military and, of course politics. Far too many.' He took a deep drag on his cigar.

'If I may ask, sir, I take it you didn't go there?'

The Prime Minister chuckled. 'No I didn't. Not bright enough. I barely scraped into Sandhurst, it took me three attempts to pass the entrance exam. And I was a dunce at Harrow. The truth is I was never asked to learn anything which seemed of the slightest use or interest to me, so I didn't bother. But the subjects that did interest me, English and history, I excelled in, although I say so myself. It was on my report card too, which provoked about the only positive reaction I got from my father in all my school days. And I was also the public schools fencing champion. The school newspaper said my success was chiefly due to my quick and dashing attack, which quite took opponents by surprise.' He nudged Griffiths. 'There will come that time again...'

After a couple of contemplative puffs on the cigar: 'And what about you young Griffiths, what's your story? A wife, hmm? A sweetheart?'

'I have a girl, Cheryl. At least I had. I haven't heard from her in weeks.'

He sat up straighter on the bench. 'We're not allowed to make any contact of course. And if she has written to me then it hasn't got to me...obviously.'

He shifted his position, slightly away from the older man.

'Hackney. She lives in Hackney. We both did. I don't know what has happened...or to my parents. My younger brother Chris hasn't come back from France, he was as fusilier, the Royals. We haven't heard.' His voice tailed off.

Churchill patted him on the top of his head with his left hand. 'We'll come through this Griffiths. I don't know when, but we will.'

65

He stood up, as if he was about to address the House of Commons, staring out into the emptiness.

'The bloody Belgians and their damnable king. If Leopold hadn't thrown in the towel and surrendered his army to the Nazis, without even discussing it with his ministers, we might have avoided the greatest British military defeat in our history. If they had held for even a few days we might have got all our lads out, your brother Griffiths'. Glancing back over his shoulder, 'And we might have been fighting them on the beaches as I said to the House. But the time will come.'

He turned around to face the young soldier. 'Again, as I vowed, we shall never surrender. Never. That was a solemn commitment. We have what remains of our air force in the north and we have our people. We are already fighting them in the streets, but not in the way they imagined, or fancy young Griffiths. We are striking them from behind, we are coming for them in the dark, creeping up on them. The soldiers we have, the men and women out of uniform, are striking and as we get more organised, as the news gets out of our successes, it will spread, mark my words. We will terrorise the Germans. They will not be safe on our streets or in their beds.'

'I heard that speech sir,' Griffiths responded.

'Mmm…Yes, this one too. Forgive me if there's any repetition,'

Churchill smiled down at his companion. 'You know when I sat down I whispered – to Attlee I think – "And we'll fight them with the butt ends of broken beer bottles, because that's bloody well all we've got." It was an exaggeration, not much of one mind you.'

He sat down beside Griffiths, letting out a slight groan as he scrunched onto the bench. 'They will never take me. If I go I will go like that.' He chuckled. 'Although it won't be the butt end of a broken beer bottle in my dead hand,' he winked at Griffiths, 'but a brandy one.'

8

The bullet glanced off a rib, breaking it, before carrying on, passing through the front of the shirt and burying in the turf. The impact of it pitched him forward and then the pain burst through and engulfed him and he passed out. When he came round he opened his eyes to fast-moving sky and as he turned his head he realised that it was him that was travelling, even through the pulsing pain he could hear voices and screams, sirens and shouted instructions, the sound of machinery, engines roaring. He was on a stretcher, he could see the back of the person at his feet carrying one end of it but when he moved to look up at the one at his head the pain surged to a crescendo and he began to slip under again. He heard a voice echoing and falling away say, 'You'll be fine son.'

That was three days ago. The pain was manageable now, no doubt due to the stuff they were banging into his veins from the drip bag on the stand next to his bed. He had lost a lot of blood, he knew that because he had watched the transfusions go in. There had been hours, he didn't know how many, when he was in a kind of delirium, semi-conscious, with figures coming and going through vapour, but now he could eat and sit up, shuffle to the edge of the bed to use a bedpan and relate to and talk to the nurses and doctors who came and went.

He had his own room, but he could hear the noise and occasional cries from the ward through the glass partition. There was a large window, he didn't know which direction it faced or what it looked onto because there were blackout curtains, but even when, occasionally, a nurse opened them, it seemed just as black, no light was getting in through the criss-cross of taping and what seemed like dark paint underneath. It was insufferably hot too, that was a bit of an exaggeration, but it caused him to sweat at night, although that could also be due to the drugs he guessed. And he was bored. There hadn't been any guests, no newspapers or books, although until today he hadn't been able to even think about reading or doing anything vaguely active. He was wearing a large smock, a hospital gown, but he could unbutton it to the waist, so that he could look at the binding over the wound which stretched around his torso, but it was lumpy, padded, over where the bullet had tracked through him. He wondered what had happened to his holed and bloody shirt. He'd have to ask. It would be a souvenir.

The door opened and a doctor came in, one he didn't recognise, but then why would he? He had a stethoscope round his neck, hanging down to his white coat, and a badge but he couldn't make out the words. They seemed smudged.

'You're looking much better,' the doctor said. 'I'm just going to whisk you down to a theatre, nothing to worry about, just to get a better look at the wound, in a more sterile environment. Ok?'

He didn't expect an answer because he was moving towards the door, making room for two men in dark blue tops, male nurses, wheeling in a trolley. The doctor, who looked to be about fifty, with thinning grey hair and a pinched face, heavy glasses and a salt and pepper moustache, pulled back the bed covers and leaned over, grasping his right arm.

'Careful now,' he said, 'take my arm for balance and I'll guide you.'

One of the nurses, again a man who looked to be in middle age, a lock of dark hair dropping onto his brow, took the other arm as the third, considerably younger, pulled the drip stand and between them eased him onto the gurney.

'Actually,' the doctor said, 'I think we can do without the drip now, it's just getting in the way.' And he pulled off the tape holding the needle and quickly slipped the needle out. 'Now lie back.'

He looked at the ceiling as they wheeled him through a ward, he could turn his head and see the filled beds with patients as he passed. In one a young man with a bandaged head even waved to him and gave him the thumbs up. He heard another shout, 'Glad you're ok,' and a couple of claps before they came to a stop at a medical lift, waiting for a few seconds until it rumbled to their floor and the doors opened, and then they were inside.

When the doors opened again they were clearly in an ill-lit basement, it smelled dusty and slightly damp.

'This isn't—-' he began to say.

'Don't worry, it's just a slight detour,' the other nurse, who spoke for the first time, said down to him as the gurney pushed through the place, wheels rattling on a rough floor. Then up a slight incline, doors creaking open and they were outside. He raised himself onto his elbows to see the open doors of an ambulance.

'Hey!' Someone called.

He looked round to see it came from a German soldier, bareheaded, who was dropping a cigarette and moving towards them.

'Was ist los?'

'We have permission,' he heard the doctor reply, moving towards the soldier and reaching inside his white coat for credentials, and then what he could only describe as three quick puffs of sound as the soldier first sat down, then toppled backwards onto the ground.

'Quick, get him inside,' the doctor said, the silenced pistol still in his right hand. Then to him, 'We're taking you to a safe place, we're with the resistance Mr Matthews…Stan. We'll make sure they can't get you. Trust me.'

Then he was inside with the three men, the ambulance kicked into life and juddered off. There were four of them of course, plus the driver.

The doctor clapped him on the shoulder. 'I really am a doctor too, although I'm more used to saving lives than taking them. You'll have the best of care Stan. You'll be back playing football sooner than you realise. And not for a prison camp team.'

'That,' Matthews replied, 'really would be a result.'

9

They glanced at each other, he motioned to her with a nod and she grasped what he meant immediately, slipping in behind the bedroom door. The pistol was in his right hand, the left on the smooth, round doorknob of the bedroom door which was slightly ajar, giving him the sliver of a view into the darkened hall. He heard the creak of a closing door, the rustle of clothing – a coat being taken off and hung up perhaps, and then, as he was turning the handle, the ringing of a bell, startling him, until he realised it must be the doorbell. He paused. Then glanced at Morris and shook his head.

A muffled voice saying, 'Professor Fuchs, a package from the university,'

The sound of the front door creaking open again and then scuffling and pitched voices he couldn't make out. He looked round at Morris, she shook her head.

There was silence now. Then a voice saying, 'I don't really want to have to shoot you Herr Fuchs, it would totally defeat the purpose of my visit. But I'll take out your knee if you don't cooperate?'

'What do you want?' Fuchs answering.

Sol could see through the crack of the door the back of a man with wavy dark hair, beyond him the indistinct shape of the other, the one who must be holding the weapon.

'In other circumstances I'd be happy to discuss that with you but all you need to know is that you are coming with me.' It was an English accent.

'No I'm not.' Fuchs.

Sol glanced at Morris. She shrugged, raising her eyebrows. He waited, his face to the crack of the door and the slanted view. He knew he couldn't throw it open because Fuchs was between him and his target. He waited.

'If you shoot me,' Fuchs in accented English, 'it will be heard all over the street and the militia will be here in minutes.'

Sol didn't know if he was bluffing and neither, apparently, did the gunman. Because there was no response. Fuchs was either very brave or he just didn't care.

It happened so fast he couldn't make it out, Fuchs back was to him and then it wasn't and now he could see the other man clearly, a gun in his right hand looking down towards the floor. Sol thought about what to do, as calmly as he could, he was aware of Morris moving away from her post and behind him. If only he had been given a silencer for the pistol.

He threw open the door, moved into a slight crouch, both hands now on his gun.

The man, who was well-built and wearing what looked like some short dark overcoat or jacket, appeared to be in his early forties, he was startled momentarily, but then recovered. Sol could see Fuchs crumpled body now, he had clearly been hit with the other man's gun. Which was now held in his right hand, almost down at his waist.

'Drop it,' he said.

The other man looked at him. 'I don't think so.' And he pulled up his gun – it registered with Sol that it was a Luger – slowly, perhaps testing whether Sol would fire, until both men were each now aiming at one another.

Afterwards he would try to recall if he had heard anything immediately before the other man seemed to cough, the gun clattered to the ground and he fell backwards, one of his legs rattling on the wooden floor. Now he could see the handle of a knife sticking from his chest, just below his throat.

Morris moved past him. 'Tend to Fuchs,' she said over her shoulder.

He watched her pull out the knife from the man's chest, then plunge it several times into the prone body before, he lost count of the blows, finally stopping, standing fully upright, then wiping the blade on her trouser leg.

Sol pocketed his gun, bent over the unconscious Fuchs, noticed a large welt on his forehead and a cut oozing blood. He put his cheek over the man's mouth and was slightly reassured when he felt breath on it.

'That was impressive,' he said, turning to Esther as she bent down beside him over Fuchs.

'Unlike you. You'd still be standing there, not knowing what to do if I hadn't saved you.'

'Gunshots would have brought the police.'

The truth was he felt extremely foolish as he looked at her. 'Where did you learn to do that?'

'I used to be a knife thrower in the circus. Reversed the stereotype and a man in tight shorts stood against the board with the balloons around him while I chucked them.'

'Really?'

'No. Is Fuchs ok?'

'Breathing. I don't know if any other damage is done. If he's wanted for his brain that wouldn't do. Give me a hand getting him to the bed. And then we can take a closer look.'

'It needs bathed. His head.'

Sol moved round and manoeuvred his arms under Fuchs' armpits, Morris grabbed his legs and they lifted and carried the unconscious scientist to the bed. Then she slipped out and came back a few seconds later with a soaked hand towel which she pressed onto the swelling on the man's forehead. Kane left her to it.

A minute or too later, with Fuchs still apparently unconscious, she came out of the bedroom. Sol was standing, looking back across the hall and to the body. He noticed that a few feet away was the dropped gun. He was right, it was a Luger. Nazi, he thought to himself.

'That's a pretty impressive doorstop,' pointing to the body, to Morris who was still holding the wet towel. 'What are we going to do about it…him?'

'Search him and see if there's any identification for a start. Then we'll think about it.'

Sol walked over to the dead man. Even in the half light the blood on the chest shone and it had also leaked from him to form a pool to one side of his body. He bent over, gingerly, unbuttoned the sodden jacket, rummaged through the pockets before going into the trouser ones. Then he unlaced the shoes and searched inside and in the socks.

'Nothing. He's a Nazi for sure,' he said over his shoulder, 'judging by the Luger he was holding. I'm sure one of ours wouldn't have been using that.' He picked up the weapon and put it in the empty pocket of his trousers. A gun at both hips. Just like John Wayne, he thought.

He realised he was talking to himself, Morris was no longer there. He got up and walked through to the bedroom. Fuchs was still out on the bed. Morris was now pulling the cloth back from his forehead.

'Ice would have been good,' she said.

'Let's hope that blow didn't permanently scramble his brains or he's useless to us.'

'So you do know what this is about?'

'No,' he replied, 'it's just obvious that whatever he's involved in is vital, or they wouldn't have sent two of us. Separately.'

She stood up and looked him in the face, she was so close she could feel her breath hitting him.

'Perhaps they just figured that you weren't up to the job. As you proved just now.'

'Sorry. I must have missed the assassination refresher course…but thank you. I was just on the point of pulling the trigger.'

'It's as well you didn't. You're right. That would have startled the neighbours, never mind the pigeons.'

She seemed to relax slightly. 'He would probably have pulled the trigger too. So, we need to get Fuchs on his feet and out of here. We don't know that there aren't others around, or arriving.'

He nodded. 'We need to move the Nazi here, hide the body from casual sight, and before rigour mortis sets in. I can't think of anywhere else but the bathtub. Ok? Be warned though, it's messy work.'

She shrugged and they moved into the hall and repeated how they had moved Fuchs, stumping along as they went, careful not to slip on the wet blood, and then swinging the body up and into the bath, head at the tap end, his feet limp and dangling over the other end of the bath.

Sol was panting slightly. 'Perhaps we should fill the bath?'

'What, so it looks like suicide?' She began to laugh.

Sol chuckled with her.

'I thought that perhaps the water would mask the smell, as he begins to rot.'

She shook her head and a fleeting smile passed her lips. 'You should have thought of that earlier and put in the plug before we dumped him.'

Sol looked down as the face of the dead man, eyes still open, staring up at him.

'Fuck it,' he said eventually, 'let's see how Fuchs is.'

He was beginning to stir, moaning slightly, as they went back into the bedroom. The wet cloth had slipped from his forehead and he was struggling to sit up. Sol pulled him up so his back was against the bedhead. His eyes were open but they looked glazed, filmy.

'We're comrades,' he said. He held up three fingers of his right hand. 'Can you see? How many are there?'

Fuchs put his right hand to his forehead, fingering the swelling. He took his hand away and looked at his own fingers, spotted with blood.

'Don't be stupid,' he said. 'What happened after he hit me?'

His accent was marked, slightly guttural, but he wasn't stumbling over words.

'He was a Nazi.' Esther said from over his shoulder. 'He wanted to take you to them. You must be very important.'

Fuchs snorted. 'I'm only a research scientist. I'm not in the least important. Do you know what it is I do?'

'No,' Sol cut in, 'and we don't want to.'

'My head is thumping, is that the right term?' Fuchs said, moving it slightly, as if concerned it might topple. 'And the man...the Nazi... what happened to him?'

'Don't worry,' Esther said, 'his Seig Heiling days are done.'

Fuchs breathed deeply, as if he couldn't take in what was being said to him 'I feel sick,' he began to move from the bed 'I need to go to the bathroom.'

'Not a good idea,' Sol pushed him back down. 'Do you have a basin or a bucket?'

'Under the sink. And in the kitchen cabinet just above there's aspirin. Could you bring that?'

Sol nodded. 'And I'll bring a glass of water.'

'You're probably concussed,' Morris came in. 'So you can rest for a bit to get your senses back. But we need to get out of here in a little while because we don't know if he was just the advance guard and more will be turning up. Do you understand?'

He nodded slowly. 'You're in the party I suppose?'

She nodded.

'Thank you then. You must be right, that this isn't safe.' He smiled slowly. 'A few hours ago I was just a research scientist and now, a few hours later, I'm a wanted man. How the world tips.'

Then: 'Can you tell me your names, is that allowed?'

She nodded, just as Sol was coming in with a basin in his two hands, inside of which he was balancing a glass of water and, beside it, a bottle of pills.

'I'm Esther,' she said, 'and he', she nodded her head, 'is Sol.'

'Here you go,' Sol placed the basin on the bed beside Fuchs. 'Is there a mop and a bucket? I need to clean up.'

'Yes,' Fuchs said, taking the glass. 'There's a cupboard in the bathroom, you'll find them in there.'

Sol nodded. 'We need to go once you feel a little better. Half an hour maximum.'

'I will need to take my papers, perhaps a suitcase.'

'No,' Esther said, 'unless you have a car?'

'Yes, a car. I have one. It's old.'

'Ok, when you've taken the aspirin and thrown up – or perhaps that should be the other way round? – you can grab what you need and we're out of here.'

Fuchs took the glass and she tipped out three tablet from the bottle.

'Haven't you got housework to do Sol?'

He nodded and left the room. He found the mop and bucket as Fuchs had said and looked to where he could fill up. The washbasin was too shallow and the corpse's head, his eyes staring sightlessly, was against the bath taps. Using both hands Sol grabbed his jacket front pulled him up slightly and then pushed him down so that he slid along the bottom of the tub and more of his legs went over the other end. He ran both taps, the water around the body began to tint pink before he manoeuvred the pail under the rushing water

10

June

She stirred the embers of the fire with a poker, reached with her left hand for a log and dropped it into the grate. The damp wood hissed as the heat took it, she dropped the long poker into the fire bucket, a battered brass artillery shell from the first war, took the coffee pot from the iron grille over the fire, settled back in the wooden chair, picked up the metal cup and poured herself another shot of the bitter coffee.

The only sounds were the metronomic clicking of the grandfather clock and the occasional slight crackles from the fire. She looked up above the mantlepiece at the black and white framed photograph of her parents, her late parents, her mother with a coy smile on her face, as if she had been given everything she had ever asked for, her father trying not to grin too broadly at the camera. Their wedding photograph. So long ago. So much in between, not much of it pleasant.

She got up, the chair creaking as she left it, and moved over to the ancient sideboard, scarred with years of use, and grabbed the brandy bottle, then put down the cup on the oak top, uncorked the bottle and slurped a measure into the coffee. She sighed, took a long gulp of the tepid mix, felt the alcohol hit her stomach, then moved back to the chair and her place in front of the fire. As she glanced around she saw that the day was beginning to emerge, the sun was coming up, bathing the whitewashed walls in a pale glow. She took another more measured sip from the cup and watched the first flames flicker as the log caught.

She hadn't slept. She had been given 48 hours to leave the house, it was being requisitioned as a billet for some German officers. There would be Deutschmarks, they told her, but she didn't want their money, she wanted nothing to do with them. Except to gloat over their deaths. She had considered setting fire to the place, depriving them of it, but they would know immediately who had done it, and she wanted to go out for more than that. She had greater ambitions.

The sun was almost up and above the tree line when she drained the last of the coffee. She got up from the chair, yawned and took a couple of paces to the side of the fireplace, picked up the shotgun, walked with it over to the dresser, took out the cleaning materials, broke the gun open and began to methodically clean it. It had been with her as far back as she could remember, so many memories of her father with it, breaking it down, polishing it, burnishing the engraved brass, picking out the hounds and ducks etched into it, walking with him as he gripped the stock on the hunt for rabbit and fowl and eventually being allowed to fire it. She couldn't have been more than ten. Now she could almost feel the kick to her shoulder as she gripped it tightly and slowly pulled the trigger, her father leaning over her as she did so.

It was always with her now, since it happened. The images kept taunting her. She grimaced and rammed the cleaning rod down one of the two barrels of the gun.

Guillaume, her father, had inherited the gun from his father, also called Guillaume. It was a St Etienne 12-gauge coach, dating from some time before World War One. Apart from the farm it was about the only thing handed down. The old man, and her grandmother, also called Eugenie, had died in the great flu pandemic, sometime in 1919. It seemed so unfair that her grand-papa had survived the war, fighting from the Somme, Ypres to the Battle of Amiens only to die of a random infection, worse than that, to bring it back with him and kill his wife.

Papa, she thought, had caught the end of the great war as a 17 year-old, demobbed in 1920 aged 20, to come back to an empty house and abandoned farm, the last one of his family, with three other children, all girls, still born and buried in the church graveyard, in the one lair, stacked one on top of the other like tiny parcels on a shelf. There it was, her father, mother and grandparents on his side all dead before they turned 40. As she probably would be.

There was the other branch of the family, long since sundered, split over mama marrying papa. He wasn't good enough for her, apparently. But she knew he was that and she had never sought to find her other grandparents and perhaps the grandchildren, somewhere near Metz, and she had no wish to. There was a cousin, a second cousin, or one twice removed, whatever that was, living in the town. But they barely knew each other enough to nod to. She was not going to go there, even if asked, unlikely as that might be.

She put down the cleaning rod, opened the dresser, retrieved the box of stubby cartridges and rammed two shells into the gun's chambers, and clicked it shut.

After it had happened, when she regained consciousness and saw her father dead beside her, she had crawled and stumbled her way into the house for the gun, but when she came out with it they were gone, of course. She didn't know why they hadn't killed her as well, and at the time she had willed it, she had put the twin barrels under her chin but somehow her hand had locked and she hadn't been able to pull the trigger. Perhaps they hadn't killed her, those three German men, boys really, because they wanted her to live with it, to recall it and, although she tried to banish it, it had worked.

It was time to do something about it.

She took the gun through to the kitchen, to the walk-in cupboard, found the sleeve for it, slid the St Etienne inside, slung the leather strap over her head so that the sheathed shotgun was on her back, and pulled her father's coat from the peg behind the door. It was huge on her, hanging loosely on her slim frame, enveloping her so that the gun case was no more than a bump on her back. She walked through to the small dining room with the full length mirror and turned slowly, looking at her reflection, particularly over her shoulder from behind. It would do, she thought.

She didn't bother locking the door. It wouldn't matter one way or the other, there was nothing more to plunder and she still had a day to move out, if she came back. She looked at her watch. It was barely 7am. From inside the barn she pulled out her bicycle and climbed on. She was wearing a pair of her father's old corduroy work pants, which she had tied with string around the ankles to stop the legs flapping into the chain, and she started pedalling, knowing exactly where she was going.

It took her half an hour to get there, as it had the four previous days. When she got to the narrow bridge over the river she dismounted, wheeled the bike into the dense undergrowth so that it couldn't be seen from the road and scrambled back to her pitch under the bridge. The river was low, the water splashed over her feet as she took off the coat, bundled it up and wedged it between a couple of rocks, and pulled the strap over her head and unsheathed the shotgun. She hadn't bothered bringing other cartridges, there was no point. There would be no time to reload if she failed. She checked that the steps she had cut into the bank were still firm and returned to her spot under the bridge, checked her watch, and settled down to wait.

She felt nothing other than a sense of purpose, there was no peace to be made, she had long since ceased to be a believer, there was no one to grieve for her, except perhaps the priest, and she tried not to think of the past, just on what she had to do.

If there was one thing to commend the Nazis, she thought, it was their organisation, discipline and timekeeping. That was dependable. The rest of it? Well that teetered on invention, temerity and pure good luck, a rocky foundation. The way she had calculated it, if it went to plan, if you could call it that, she had around twenty minutes to get away, which was plenty of time – if nothing else entered the stage, like a lorry full of soldiers, or an armoured car, or even a local waltzing past on the way for bread or absolution. She looked at her watch again. Ten minutes.

It was the perfect spot, the road snaked around the hills, a succession of tight corners forcing the changing down of gears and a reduction in speed, before the last buttress and then the hard left onto the narrow bridge and the crawl over the river. It wasn't wide enough for two cars to pass. One coming in one direction had to stop for another coming the other way, although there was no agreed etiquette, just mutual road politeness. Which still existed in these times, although she didn't imagine a German car or halftrack would observe it. There had been talk of knocking the bridge down and building a new one quickly, so the armour could pass in both directions, but so far they hadn't got round to it.

Five minutes.

For some reason she thought of the English airman, then she remembered he was Scottish, barely older than her, sawing his parachute straps away and him dropping like a limbless dummy to the ground, and then dragging him in, cutting off his flying clothes and bathing his wounds, trying not to look down to his his naked groin, the memories of what had happened before too vivid.

Now she heard the heard the low sound of the approach. She knew the engine noise would be amplified by the narrow gully, but they were close. She quickly pulled on the coat and moved out from under the bridge to the bank and the steps, the shotgun held in her two hands.

The engine whined briefly as the driver moved down a gear, and now she was moving up the steps in the bank quickly as the motorbike and sidecar emerged from around the rocky corner. She waited until it was almost on her before she raised the gun. Her target was travelling so slow that she could not miss. She fired one barrel and then the other.

Later, and in dozing at night, she believed she had seen the looks of surprise on their goggled faces and then the explosions of blood as the metal sprays hit them. But not at the time. Just the bike slowing and finally coming to rest against a stanchion of the bridge, the motor still running. That was the only sound. She couldn't even hear the gurgling of river water, just the ticking over of the motorcycle, barely heard against the roaring in her ears.

As she stood clutching the gun, looking at the two slumped figures in grey, she expected to feel some kind of emotion, remorse or guilt, but she only felt satisfaction for having executed, that was the right word, the job. And then the rush of being unexpectedly alive.

She had worked out previously that they must be messengers, running between Morlaix and Brest, so she dashed quickly to the two corpses and the wedged bike still turning over. It seemed to butt against the bridge, trying to move forward, and she realised it was still in gear. She reached beyond the driver who had now slumped on top of his comrade and switched off the engine. Then she pulled the driver back up. His face was unrecognisable, a flattened shiver of blood, his throat still slowly pumping it out. She carefully placed the shotgun on the ground and then took a Luger pistol out of its holster around the driver's waist and grasped it in two hands. Then she went to the passenger's side and the other one, an officer she could tell by the shoulder markings. His uniform, at the chest, was pockmarked by patches of blood where the shot had caught him, he still had on his peaked hat, but it was on the back on his head, almost as if he was in the middle of taking it off, but a wound on his forehead had curtailed it. She heard wheezing and realised he was still alive. She paused for a moment, she savoured it afterwards, pulled up the Luger, thumbed back the safety catch, rammed it between his teeth and blew the back of his head off.

Then she pushed him away, searched down inside the cockpit, found a leather briefcase next to the officer's feet, pulled it out and dropped it in the road. Then the machine pistol which was still in his lap.

For a second or two she wondered what to take and what to discard, the briefcase was crucial and the pistol, the machine gun too. Then she heard the sound of a vehicle and as she turned, pulling up the sub-machine gun, she saw that there was a car approaching from the other side of the bridge. It was black, low slung, it wasn't a military one she could tell even from distance. She waved and then pointed repeatedly at it, and then made a pushing motion with the palm of her hand, urging the driver to move back.

After several seconds she heard the crunch of gears engaging, the car moved slowly backwards and the headlights blinked that the message was understood.

She got back to collecting what she could, what was necessary.

11

Kreisler picked up the buzzing phone. 'Yes'

'Ober Klopp is asking for an urgent meeting, sir' Gerta, his secretary replied.

'Did he say what it's about?'

'No sir. Just that he had to see you urgently. He's with me now. He seems, hmm, quite agitated.'

Kreisler leaned back in the swivel chair and tossed the paperknife he was cleaning his nails with onto the desk. 'Very well, send him in.'

Klopp was one of the few men on his staff who had been involved in frontline fighting and had taken a light wound to his back when a British or French shell had exploded a few yards from him and he caught a shred of shrapnel. In Kreisler's judgment he was unhappy at being reposted to an essentially administrative position.

The door opened and Klopp took three quick steps across the wooden floor, clicked his heels and threw up his arm in salute. 'Heil Hitler.'

'Yes, yes Gerhardt, stand at ease. You may take a chair if you wish.'

'Thank you sir,' he replied, 'but I prefer to stand. I won't detain you for long.'

'Fine,' Kreisler pulled his chair closer to the desk. 'I can't offer you coffee or anything?'

'No, thank you.'

'Well, go on. What is it that's so urgent?'

Klopp was a Berliner. He was bareheaded, cropped dark hair, a gaunt expressionless face. Kreisler put him at about 24, in a hurry and with ambition to rise quickly. There were so many of them striving so desperately to be noticed and pushed up the ladder.

'It's Beck. He didn't report for duty this morning and no one seems to know where he is.'

'Really?' Kreisler sat up straight in his chair, at full attention now. 'That's not like him. No, not at all. He isn't ill is he?'

Klopp shook his head stiffly. 'No sir. We checked where he was staying, at that hotel. As far as we can tell – from the account from the hotel staff, his male servant principally – he left his room in the early evening and didn't come back. His bed hasn't been slept it.'

'And this servant, what did he say? When did he last see him?'

'He said that he had prepared Beck's dress uniform, sponged it and ironed it. That the obergruppenführer seemed to be in a very cheerful mood before he went out.'

'Didn't say where he was going?'

'No sir.'

'Didn't ask?'

'No he didn't. He said that he felt that was not his business, that the obergruppenführer…would no doubt have been extremely angry had he done so—-'

'Indeed he would. Did Beck say when he would be back?'

'Apparently not.'

'Anything else?'

90

'Just that the fellow, Dupont I think is his name, Albert, felt that the obergruppenführer must have had some appointment. He assumed it must have been military.'

'But of course it wasn't?'

'No sir.'

'Nothing more?'

Klopp again shook is head. His posture seemed to have relaxed slightly.

'His leaving the hotel was confirmed by a waitress who was tidying in the lobby. Well, she didn't know Beck's name. But she said she did see a German officer leaving, she thought, about 7pm. Which fits with the servant's account.'

Kreisler raised his head towards the flaking ceiling and sighed. 'This Dupont fellow, what do we know about him.'

'Almost nothing. He has worked there for several months. He had a small shop in the main street before. He was apparently excused military service for his age, a previous wound and some sight condition.'

'Blind eye.'

'Pardon?'

'Nothing Klopp, go on. Have you brought him in for interrogation?'

'We've had him for four hours. He's been questioned several times, including by me, but his story doesn't change.'

'Family? A point of weakness?'

'Yes, well no. He has a wife and three children but apparently they left for somewhere in the south months ago. They seem to have split up acrimoniously. We're trying to verify that. He lives in the hotel and we've searched his room thoroughly but there's nothing suspicious there.'

Kreisler stood up and brushed his hands down his uniform, which he did almost as a habit.

'Dammit,' he spat it out, 'we're stretched enough as it is without mounting any kind of search. You don't think he could be holed up in some woman's bed and…no, he's too efficient and punctilious to do that. He knows his duty.'

He moved out from behind the desk and started to walk slowly towards the door, forcing Klopp to wheel round to follow him, then turned on his heel and came back to within a couple of feet of the younger man.

'Let's not appear to be too worried about him missing. Can you rustle up a few uniforms, say a dozen, and try to trace his movements. Knock a few doors, a few likely places, bars, halls, I don't know…and then if he doesn't come back before nightfall we'll have to ratchet it up a bit, loudspeakers, lights, that kind of thing. And tomorrow, God forbid, if he still hasn't been seen we'll have to organise a proper search party.'

Klopp snapped his heels. 'Of course. I'll get to that right now, with your permission?'

'On you go,' Kreisler said, 'Oh and perhaps…' causing Klopp to pause halfway to the door and turn to face his superior, '…perhaps get hold of a picture of Beck in case we have to put up a missing poster.' He shook his head. 'How embarrassing would that be? And also give an order that no soldier of any rank is to go into town unaccompanied. At least three strong. No breaching of the local maidenhood, if there is such a thing? At least for the time being. Clear?'

The door clicked shut behind Klopp. Kreisler walked to the window. From this first floor of the Mairie he had a fine view along to the start of the houses in the town, with their tiled roots, and long chimneys, just as they would have been two hundred years before. It looked so peaceful.

'Peaceful my arse,' he said to himself. This, on top of the assassination of Dubois, which of course no one had the faintest idea about who could have done it.

'The peasants are rising are they?' He said softly to the glass. 'Well we'll see about that.'

12

August

'You realise,' Fuchs said in thickly-accented English, 'when they find the body they'll think that I'm the murderer.'

Kane had given him an edited version of the events which had passed, and the life taken, when he was unconscious on the floor.

'Better that than the victim,' Morris replied. 'Because at best you'd be wearing stripes in a labour camp with your fingernails missing, working on your scientific experiments, whatever they are, and at worst you'd be the scientific experiment as the Nazis took your body apart, organ by organ.'

'I'm not sure you two are much better.'

They were standing in the lounge of Fuchs' flat, one provided by the university, which was spartanly furnished. It was clear that the scientist spent little time there. There was a gas fire, a table with a radio, a standard lamp, a threadbare rug and a mismatched armchair and sofa which might have been fashionable when the old king was on the throne, but were now stained and lumpy with a few equally mismatched cushions. That was it. The overhead light didn't even have a shade.

'You will,' Fuchs' pronounced it *vill*, 'have to tell me again exactly who you are and what you want with me. I am confused.'

'I'm Kane and this is Morris. Sol and Esther We've been sent by the party to collect you and keep you safe.'

Fuchs was holding a wet cloth to the side of his forehead where he had been hit.

'You'd better sit down before you fall down,' Morris said.

Fuchs nodded and stumbled a little giddily to the armchair. 'Where are we going?' he said.

'Well?' Morris said, looking at Kane.

'How much petrol is in your car?' Kane said to Fuchs.

'I don't know, perhaps a half of a tank? A hundred miles at most?'

'Well that's where we're going,' Kane responded.

'And that's the plan?' Morris shook her head. 'Drive until the petrol runs out?'

'You're not helping Morris.'

'Well I did just a few minutes ago. Your life is now mine, to do what I want with it, given it's forfeited to me since I saved it.'

'You're being a little dramatic.'

'You two were staring at each other like gunfighters from a movie and it took a woman to change the script,' she said.

'OK,' he said reluctantly, 'I do owe you and I'm grateful.'

'Beholden.'

'Very…grateful.'

'Do you two,' Fuchs said, 'even like each other? You're probably married, you sound like you are.'

'We only met this evening,' Kane replied. 'It was just instant, mutual antipathy.'

He nudged Morris in the ribs, more forcefully than friendly, so that she grunted. 'We're hoping to nurture it so that it will develop into full-blown hatred.'

'Already there,' Morris came back. 'Keep up Kane.'

Fuchs took down the compress from his head. 'You too are meant to be comrades,' he said wearily. 'I don't know much about your business, but it would help if you got on, or at least pretended to. I'd feel a lot more secure.'

Kane looked at Morris, she shrugged. 'That's a fair point.'

'All right' she said, 'we'll do that. We'll try. Fuchs, Klaus, you get whatever you need, your papers, notes, whatever makes you operational elsewhere. And just a few clothes. An overnight bag.'

'Meanwhile,' Kane added, 'Esther and I will put our heads together and, not banging them, come up with the best way from here. We'll get instructions from the centre too.'

Fuchs nodded and slowly got up from the armchair. 'It's not like I've got much choice.'

'Positive thinking Klaus. Get your stuff. And if you need to go to the toilet,' Morris said to his back, 'well I wouldn't '

When he had left Kane stood up, quickly followed by Morris, as if there could be no advantage one to the other. 'He's right,' he said, 'we have to co-operate and also not bicker in front of him.'

'Oh, I was enjoying it.'

'And I do owe you my life. If you hadn't stepped in it would probably be double-parking in the bath now.'

She nodded. 'At least we got Fuchs before they did. We'll need to tell London.'

'I know. I'll call – or you can – how's that for co-operation? And we need to get him to a safe place. I don't fancy trying to drive back south, risking the shifting roadblocks, not knowing who's in control. The war is moving so fast we don't know where's been taken, where's safe. Best to presume nowhere is. Do you agree?'

'Yeah. But at least part one is accomplished. But he's right, Fuchs. When that body begins to ripen or when he doesn't turn up at work then they'll come here and he'll be a murder suspect. It won't just be the Nazis looking for him.'

'We can't call the police and we don't know if the resistance here has been infiltrated or not. I don't want to take that chance.' Morris nodded. 'Trust no one. We're on our own.'

'I'm sure you're used to that.'

'Like you.'

'Like me.'

'Now we have to interact.' He held out his hand to her and she took it and they shook. 'That knife trick was very impressive. How did you really learn it?'

'Is this relevant?' She shook her head.

'No, just interested. If you don't want to tell me that's fine. It's just curiosity. It's not every day you owe your life to a circus act.'

She smiled for the first time. 'I was about eleven or twelve and my parents sent me to some awful school in the wilds of Northumberland. It was girls only and I was bullied constantly for the first term, led by a an older fat kid called Honore Abelman. There was always a pack around her taking their cue from her, or willing her to go further. I was their target. For night after night I cowered and snivelled under my blankets and then one day I decided that anything was better than this. I'm simplifying I know. Perhaps I just grew courage.'

'Go on.'

'I stole a bone handled kitchen knife one night, got up early every day, usually about five, and went for a walk. At least that's what I would have told anyone who had asked me what I was doing. I had the knife down my knickers against my leg under the skirt. There was a wood on the edge of the school and I had a target tree and I practised throwing. It's not too difficult, even without a proper throwing knife, if you do it correctly. With a balanced knife like now it's simple.'

'I don't suppose you want to tell me where you keep it now.'

She shook her head. 'Nowhere you'll find anyway.'

She rubbed the side of her face as if easing an old sore. 'We had to play cricket. A bloody stupid game. But it gave me an excuse to practise throwing. Not just the ball. Stones, usually. I could throw further than any girl in the school. I also have great hand-eye coordination.'

'Deadly. I saw. What happened to Honore.'

'We were playing some other school at cricket. She was the wicket keeper, because she was blubbery and couldn't run. I was fielding and I knew the ball would come to me eventually. It did. I was about 20 yards away and I threw it at her head. Hard. If she had had any hand-eye coordination she would have caught it, or at least moved her fat arse out of the way. But I hit her right on the forehead, on target, and she dropped like she'd been shot. Of course I started screaming and crying and saying "Sorry, sorry. It was an accident. Sorry." She was unconscious for minutes with me going through this tearful act of contrition when really I was stifling laughter.'

She paused, grinned. 'Obviously I thought about the knife but it was a bit far away and there were too many witnesses.'

'She recovered and that was the end of it?'

'Not quite. About a week later, when her head was still black and blue and swollen like a giant rotting pumpkin I sneaked into the dorm room she shared with three other girls. She was on her back, snoring. I sliced the pillow on both sides of her head and crept out. She got the blame for it but she knew it was me. Next time I saw her I did the throat-cutting gesture, just to reinforce the message. That was the end of it. She wasn't there next term.'

'I don't know whether to be impressed or frightened.'

Esther smiled. 'Both.'

The sound of the door opening made them both instinctively turn, and Fuchs came in, struggling to carry a suitcase in both hands.

'I thought I said essentials,' Kane said.

'I hope it's a big car,' Morris followed up.

Fuchs dropped it on the floor. 'Most of it is files. Research work. I don't suppose you want me to junk those.'

'Anything you need from the university?' Morris was scratching her nose with the back of her index finger.

Fuchs shook his head. 'No, I copied everything. No one will be able to understand my notes anyway.' He seemed to shiver. 'I had to go to the bathroom. I thought I was going to throw up....you two frighten me.'

'We're the two who will keep you safe,' Kane said, 'remember that. Otherwise you'll be working from a Nazi cell with the certainty of being shot when your usefulness runs out. You are a communist. They especially hate communists.'

'And Jews,' Morris added.

Fuchs nodded tentatively. 'I know. My parents were Lutheran.'

'They'll get to them too,' she said.

'Let's go,' Morris said. 'Take us to the car.'

13

'How did you get this?'

'That's not important,' the priest responded. 'What it says is.'

'What did he say?' Mac asked.

'We can speak in English,' Pierre Baudin said.

'I can translate for Genie if necessary,' Coyle smiled at the girl beside him.

The four of them were sitting around a card table in the priest's small drawing room. Baudin had the papers spread out in front of him.

He looks to be of enlistment age, Mac thought. But perhaps teachers had been excluded from the draft?

Baudin looked up, as if he could hear it. He was in his late thirties, hair beginning to go bald at the crown, the rest spilling untidily down and over his collar. Occasionally he ran a hand through it to put it back in place as he bent over the paper in front of him.

'This could get us all shot.'

'You're stating the obvious,' the priest responded. 'What do you make of it?'

Mac was staring across the table at Genie and she was returning it without expression. Her hair was swept back from her face into a knotted headscarf at an angle on her head. There was a smudge of dirt

101

under her right eye and he had to restrain himself from reaching across the table to rub it off. She continued to look at him and he wondered what she was thinking. He wondered if it was about him. He smiled slightly, but she did not respond. This woman had saved his life, he thought, no doubt about it, and he didn't know how to thank her properly. If the Nazis discovered what she'd done they'd shoot her, if she was lucky. She must have known that, he thought, and she risked it for me. Another voice in his head came in, don't kid yourself, it was just hatred of the Nazis.

The three others sat in silence, waiting on the teacher to read the papers and provide a translation. A clock ticked in the background, the framed prints on the wall were all of village scenes, markets, churches, people, women in bonnets, men is sturdy tweeds. There was no religious iconography on the walls. Mac wondered if that meant something.

Eventually the teacher looked up. 'Most of it is very dull, about duties and shifts and requests for different postings, but there is one you'll find interesting. The transfer of some allied prisoners, officers it says, eight of them who may be intelligence staff, for interrogation in Brest. French officers.'

'When?' Mac cut in.

'Tomorrow. They're being held in the town hall in Guingamp. Leaving at 8am with an escort, obviously.'

Coyle translated for Genie. She nodded her head slowly.

'You're thinking what I'm thinking,' Mac said to Coyle. 'That we need to interfere if we can. Please translate.'

The priest did so. Once again she nodded her head slowly and turned to look at Mac.

'I have to know how she got these documents,' Mac said. 'If they're genuine. This isn't making sense to me and it's dangerous.'

Coyle stood up and motioned to Genie to follow him. As they reached the door he shouted over his shoulder. 'Thank you Baudin, I think you can go now. Travel safely.'

The teacher got up, nodded to Mac, and followed them through the door.

Almost immediately the priest and the girl were back in, Coyle scrambling to pick up the documents.

'Quick, there's a German staff car and a lorry with soldiers at the bottom of the hill coming up. You and Genie need to get to the grave. Keep low as you do. Quick, they'll be here in a couple of minutes.'

Mac grabbed Genie's hand, and pulled her, she whirled round and with her free hand slapped out at him. 'Nazis,' he said into her face. 'Vite.' It was almost the last of the few French words he knew.

He thought about lighting a candle. It was pitch dark. Quiet as the grave he thought to himself and smiled. He could feel her breath on the side of his cheek as they sat on the camp bed. They were sealed off from above in the tomb but he didn't know whether the smell from a candle might leak out and alert the Germans. Then he remembered the torch the priest had given him which he'd stowed under the bed, he slid onto his knees, fumbled under for it, pushed the pistol aside, felt it but he knocked it so that it rolled and then he grasped it and pulled it out before sitting back down again on the bed.

'Torch,' he said, quietly and rather stupidly, before switching it on. He turned it onto her face briefly, then to his, then aimed it at the stone floor so that the light bounced and when he turned to look at her she was faint and ghostly.

'An odd place for a first date,' he muttered to himself. 'Sitting on a bed with a beautiful woman in the dark, it ought to be romantic and lead to, well, the obvious…but instead we're buried in the earth in a tomb and—'

He felt a nudge in the ribs, turned to face her, she was holding an index finger to her lips, telling him to be quiet. He nodded his head, whispered into her ear, 'Sorry, nervous,' knowing she wouldn't understand but feeling he had to say it anyway.

The truth was he did feel nervous, his stomach was roiling. It wasn't the threat of discovery or the fear of not getting out, or claustrophobia, it wasn't the kind of fear like being in a glass bubble as tracer fire sought you out, it was sitting next to this young woman, who smelled faintly of soap and who seemed calm and clearly did not feel the way he was feeling.

'You are beautiful,' he said in a whisper.

Neither of them said anything as the minutes passed. He wondered what was going on above with the Germans, whether it was some kind of raid. Had Coyle been taken away? If he had would they make him talk, surely they would? How long should they stay here before coming out, or, worse, being discovered if it had been forced out of Coyle. Mac glanced at his service watch and he saw from the luminous dial that they had been down here for almost an hour. How long to give it before going out?

He had switched off the torch to conserve the battery but now he pulled it up from the bed between them and turned it on again, shielding the beam with his right hand. Genie had her head back against the stone wall behind, she turned to face him and smiled. He realised that was the first time he had seen her smile at him. It was a knowing smile, he thought, as if she was keeping something to herself and relishing it.

He heard a noise above, the door of the crypt above creaking. He switched off the torch and grabbed under the bed for the handgun.

He could feel her tense, afraid, like him, that they had been given up, but from the dark above the priest was saying, 'They've gone now. It's safe, come out.'

Mac let her go first and followed up the step and into what was now dusk. The air smelled clean and slightly scented, of grass, or flowers, or both. Or perhaps it was just the contrast with the stale air of the grave. Then he wondered if it was just a memory of the scent that Genie had given off.

'What did they want?' He said to Coyle as they stood on the gravel between the graves.

'Just routine, or at least that's what they said it was. The officer spoke French. They were after information. Apparently some German officer has disappeared and they're looking for him. House to house searches, that kind of thing. I asked if they wanted to look around, but he said that wasn't necessary. His men were outside, checking around I suppose. I offered the officer coffee, Schmidt his name was, from Frankfurt. He accepted and we agreed what a terrible thing war was and how we must settle differences, get along, restore peace...I'll have to make confession about my lying when I can find a confessor. We finished coffee, he shook my hand and asked me to pass on anything that might help recover the poor missing soul. He left a card. When he left I lit a candle and burned it. Anyway, you two, did you get better acquainted?'

He was smiling.

'Enough father,' Mac said, 'we have plans to make don't we?'

The priest nodded. 'Some of the lads are coming up shortly. We'll go inside and wait for them.' He turned and began walking away.

Mac started to follow and above the crunch of the stones under his feet he heard, from behind, 'Beautiful..'

And when he turned and looked back Genie was smiling at him and slowly shaking her head. It was the second time she had smiled.

Coyle motioned to him to come out. Six men and Genie were crammed into the small room looking at maps and talking animatedly. The air was thick with pungent tobacco smoke. Mac left them, joined the priest in the wood-panelled hall which was overseen by a large crucifix looking down at them

'It's Genie,' the priest said, 'she's been very stupid. Hot-headed.'

'Tell me.'

'The documents, the German orders, it was her who got them.'

'You're not serious.'

'Afraid so. She told me, not in the confessional, I'm sure she's not religious, but openly. In confidence of course. She handed me the packet and said she thought it might be important. It was in German, she said. I opened the heavy envelope and it was obvious right away that it came from the military, all crests and seals. I was stunned, I asked her where she got this. She was reluctant at first, but then it came out. She said she had ambushed two German soldiers in a motorcycle sidecar and discovered it.'

'Ambushed,' Mac's astonishment was obvious. 'How could she do that?'

'About five miles from here the Brest road takes a dogleg to cross a small bridge, traffic has to slow down almost to stop. She hid under the bridge and when the sidecar was about to turn onto it she popped up and fired her father's shotgun at them at point bank range. They wouldn't have had time to respond..'

'My god. She did that? How was she, talking about it?'

'Very calm. She said she didn't regret it at all, she wasn't asking for forgiveness, and that she considered it justified as retaliation against an occupying army. She didn't call it revenge, but that must have been the major part of it.'

Mac let it sink in. He felt a mixture of shock and admiration.

'She said,' Coyle continued, 'that she felt as much a soldier as any man and was as capable.'

'What did you say?'

'I told her it was foolhardy, that she couldn't act as a lone wolf, that everything had to be cleared through the resistance. That there had to be organisation. She agreed, well at least I think she did.'

'And about the German soldiers. No remorse at all.'

The priest sighed. 'Not obviously. She asked me what I thought about it, was it right? I said that God would be the judge, and she laughed.'

'God seems to have deserted us father. Or perhaps he's on the other side?'

Coyle sighed once more. 'Not you too Mac. '

He looked away, then up at the crucifix nailed to the wood next to a clock which clearly had not been wound in months, then back. 'But I agree it's difficult to see God's purpose in this.'

Mac said nothing, but briefly put his right hand on the priest's shoulder.

Coyle went on, 'I'm worried about her. The farm is being requisitioned by the Germans and she has no relatives here. So I've asked her to move in here, to be my housekeeper until...until, well who knows.'

'Is that wise Padraig? People will talk.'

'Well let them. There are much more important matters to talk about.'

Mac nodded, trying to look serious and concerned, but inside he was pleased that he would be so close to her. She hadn't given him the slightest encouragement, and you couldn't call one brief and one mocking smile that, but perhaps that was part of the attraction.

Attracted, he said in his head, to a remorseless killer? Then, who am I to judge? Just because I haven't looked my victims in the eyes, delivering it from a plane floating thousands of feet above them doesn't give me the right of judgment. It's war. All's fair. And there still is love. Somewhere.

'You're right,' he said to priest. 'We have to support each other. Now let's go back and join the war council.'

14

He pulled up the binoculars once more, scanning the road below, then to the hillside a quarter of a mile away, looking for the signal. He had been lying in the bivouac for over an hour, the sun had emerged over the trees which had provided shade, now it was beating on his back and on the beret he had pulled back on the crown of his head. It was months since he had handled a rifle, not since basic training, and then not too often, probably because they thought, why would an airman need to be proficient with one? It lay beside him, a bolt action Lebel he hadn't been able to fire in preparation, but he had loaded it and stripped it several times and he was confident that he could get shots off quickly. Hitting the target was the issue, and then reloading ten cartridges, which he prayed would not be necessary. In his jacket pocket he had a dozen more rounds.

There had been almost no traffic since they'd arrived, a couple of farm vehicles only, beaten-up old lorries belching diesel fumes, it was as if people knew what was going on and had locked themselves inside their homes, or perhaps it was that they didn't want to come up against their invaders. At one point six planes flew over, he identified them as Heinkel bombers, and then it went quiet again, just the light wind rustling the leaves on the bushes around him.

A wasp buzzed around his face, he felt it landing on his beret, he shook his head and it flew off. Mosquitoes had attacked his hands which itched incessantly, but he knew better than to scratch them. He pulled up the binoculars again, trying to pick out his colleague across on the facing hillside, or those below. They were too well camouflaged.

Still nothing.

As he understood it messages had been sent village-to-village and back to them about the progress of the small convoy. He now knew that there were four vehicles, plus the motorcyclist in front, an open lorry with two men manning a machine gun, two in the staff car, driver and an officer, the closed lorry with two in the front and the prisoners locked in behind, then the last one, another open lorry with another six soldiers in it. He counted thirteen in all, unless there was another locked inside with the French officers. And they were seven, plus Genie. Not great odds. He just hoped the others were better shots than he had been in training.

He needed a pee but that would have to wait. His stomach was alive with tension, he rolled to his left and picked up the canteen and took a quick mouthful of water, rinsed it round his dry mouth and spat it out. A buzzing in his right ear told him another mosquito was about, he raised a hand brushed it away and when he looked back to the hill above he didn't need the binoculars to catch the signal. Two pigeons rose out of the tangle of vegetation and then, just to make sure that the it hadn't been missed, he caught a glimpse of André standing and waving his arms before hunkering down again. That meant that within a couple of minutes they'd arrive.

He pulled up the Lebel against his shoulder and now below, on cue, the horse-drawn farm trailer pulled out onto the narrow road. It was piled high with brushwood and grass cuttings, there was no back to it so it left a small green and brown trail as it moved slowly along the baked tarmac, Genie holding the reins of the massive brown Breton draft horse, pulling it back rather than encouraging it forward. The trailer was now stationary, blocking the road.

The motorcycle was first to arrive. Mac had discarded the binoculars and pulled up the rifle but he could hear the soldier shouting, although he couldn't make out what he was saying it was obvious, he wanted the contraption off the road. Genie was gesticulating at him and he could hear her voice in counterpoint. He knew that she'd be apologising, saying that she didn't understand German, that she'd be as quick as she could. She was standing up now, she had dropped the reins and the horse was impatiently jerking its head up and down. The soldier got off his bike and put it on its stand, still shouting furiously, his right hand pointing and jabbing at her.

Round the bend behind him the machine gun lorry appeared and pulled up behind the bike, then the staff car, the prisoner lorry and, finally, the soldiers in the open one. A dark uniformed Gestapo officer was climbing out of the car to join in the belabouring, he guessed, as he gripped the rifle tight to his shoulder and sighted.

The grass in the back of the trailer erupted as the two men he knew as Philippe and Paul came out from under cover and began letting off the rounds, one from a pistol, the one he knew as Paul with the captured German machine pistol, at the standing and unprepared machine gunners. A chatter of fire. And now he was pulling the trigger

112

at the rear detachment, levering back the bolt, the brass spinning away, firing again.

He glanced at where Genie was, he saw the Gestapo man was flat on the ground on his back, motionless, the two resistance fighters were on board the first lorry at the machine gun. As he was told to do he kept firing at the rear lorry, bullets ripping into metal and glass, André was shooting at them from behind, the other two men, hidden on the opposite hillside were raking their targets. The noise was deafening, waves of ear-aching explosions, whining ricochets, he kept pulling back the bolt and firing until all the rounds were gone. Then he rummaged in his pockets for more ammunition and quickly pushed five or six cartridges into the breech.

There were only occasional shots as he got to his feet and began stumping down the hillside through the bracken, rifle ready at his waist to pull up. There hadn't been one return shot as far as he could tell. He raised the rifle as he approached the last lorry, which leaked water and oil from the engine, windows shattered, glass crunching under his feet, ragged holes in the bodywork and, in the cabin, the slumped shape of the driver. It had all taken place within a couple of minutes at most.

The others were in the road now, he nodded at André who had shouldered his rifle and was pointing it at where just a few seconds before men had stood. Mac noticed that the lorry was listing towards him, rounds had taken out the double tyres at the back. Cutting through the ammonia smell of cordite was that of petrol, leaking from the punctured tank and dribbling into the road.

'Vite, vite,' someone was shouting as they began to pick up the discarded German weapons. Philippe, his long coat swirling, got to work on the door of the prison truck with bolt cutters. Mac climbed onto the wheel arch of the guard truck, as did Andre at the other side. Someone was moaning in the tangle of grey bodies on the floor of the truck, Andre pulled out a pistol and began to fire carefully into the shapes. The moaning stopped.

Now the prison van was open and the men inside were coming out, looking bemused as they stood on the ground. One was holding his left arm and his hand was bloodied.

'He must have been caught by a ricochet.' Mac said out loud, to no one who could understand.

The men, still in their soiled uniforms, were being shepherded off the road to where the cars were hidden and the two old lorries. Then he saw that coming out of the back of the Mercedes lorry, where the prisoners had been, was another figure, a young German soldier with his hands up. There seemed to be just a moment's silence and then shots rang out, he didn't see who fired, and the soldier pitched back onto the ground.

Mac made his way along the edge of the carnage, stepping over the dead Gestapo officer who had been hit in the head and, it looked, by at least a couple of rounds to the body, his tunic torn open and bloody flesh glistening underneath.

Genie was standing beside the trailer, most of the grass now out and around her feet. She was wearing a heavy woollen jumper and soiled green work pants, her hair loose, around her face, a pistol down by her side, held in her right hand. She was staring into space, lost somewhere, or in shock.

A shout from behind, 'Nous devons partir.'

He stepped up to her and, still holding the rifle in his left hand, hugged her with the other, feeling a great wash of relief.

15

August

'I'm sorry to disturb you sir, but I have a rather unusual request by someone to see you. Right away. She says it's of national importance.'

Dieter von Brummer looked up from his papers, and shook his head. 'Don't they all say that Fiona?'

His eyes were sore from squinting at the tiny typing and virtually indecipherable scrawls on the pages. Or perhaps it came from the series of cigarettes he had smoked, the evidence of which was now piled up in the ashtray. He leaned back, the chair creaked as he did so.

'Who is she and what's so nationally significant?'

'She claims she's a Lady Castlerosse. She won't say what it's about, sir, she insists she'll only tell you. But she has brought a most unusual calling card.'

'Yes?'

'I'll fetch it.'

Mueller watched her wobble in her tight skirt and back towards the door and he felt a stirring in his neglected groin. Later perhaps.

The hinged door had swung shut and almost immediately opened again as his secretary backed in carrying, what seemed to be flat package, loosely wrapped in brown paper.

'It's a painting. Just that. It's been vetted and cleared.'

Von Brummer sat up in the chair. He glanced quickly around at the hung flag on the wall and the portrait of Hitler, as if asking for approval.

'Show me,' he said.

Fiona Blackett was English, not a rose exactly, her freshness had gone, if it had ever been there. She was tall and athletic, at least she was able to achieve some remarkable positions in bed which must have come with intense practice, she was the daughter of some belted earl, he recalled, a very committed Mosleyite, and now she stood at the other side of the walnut desk, peeling back the brown paper, letting it fall to the polished floor. Then she levered the picture with both hands so that it was facing him.

'It's her. Quite a good likeness.'

Von Brummer stared at it. His taste in art, such as it was, embraced the old masters, Rembrandt particularly. Well he had one, picked up from an old Jew outside Bordeaux who was trying to hide it in his attic, and he shipped it back to his study in Mainz. One for after the war to look at and allow him to relax.

This one seemed to be a fairly crude effort, a watercolour he thought, of a woman in a pink top lying on a green sofa looking towards the painter, with a tall, flowering shrub almost arching over her. On the right, open shutters framing French windows.

'You say that's her?' He squinted at it.

The woman in the picture, on a couch, propped up by cushions, had blonde hair, a parting to the left and curls brushing her ears. She was expressionless, dark red lips, fierce eyes staring out. But what drew him was her long, naked, slender legs stretched out on the sofa.

'Mmh,' he whispered.

'Do you see the signature? She says Churchill painted it in France and gave it to her. It's her. Castlerosse.'

He peered at it. 'Well,' he said, 'prop it up on the chair right by the window there and let's see what she wants...Oh, and just make sure she has been searched.'

He tidied the papers on his desk, considered whether he should remain seated, decided against it, stood up and walked a couple of paces across the wooden floor, staring at the picture. The legs. Then turned after a few seconds or so as the door opened, and Fiona ushered in the woman who was quite certainly the one in the painting..

'Sir, Lady Castlerosse.'

He clicked his heels, 'I am—'

'Oh I know who you are,' she waved her right arm airily, as if dismissing Fiona. She was wearing a small hat, almost a skull cap, a silver brooch at the front, at an angle over her left forehead, a white silk scarf, wound around her neck, below that was what he assumed was a mink jacket and below that, on those legs, he was slightly disappointed to see, baggy great harem pants. He nodded to himself. Yes, that was what they were. He couldn't see the shoes below the folds of the fabric of the trousers.

She held out her left hand and he was a little surprised that it was ringless. 'And please, call me Doris.'

He took it, bent his head brushed the back of her hand with his lips. 'Of course,' he said. 'You can call me Dieter', pointing to the leather sofa. 'Please,' he said. 'Not like the one in the painting I'm afraid.'

She glanced round, took a few steps to her right and sat down, taking time to cross those long legs in what he knew was a practised move. He leaned back onto the edge of the desk, ensuring that he was looking down at her.

'Can I offer you tea, or coffee? It's the real thing. Quite good.

'Your English is very good,' a brief smile. 'No, thank you. Not for the moment.'

He nodded slowly and let the silence grow, but she did not move into it.

'What is this about?' He broke first.

'Winston...the Prime Minister, although he wasn't then, painted that of me in 1933 on the French Riviera. At the Chateau de l'Horizon. It's owned, or at least it was, by a mutual friend, Maxine Elliott. She's an actress.'

'Go on.'

'I was married at the time, although not very firmly, to Valentine... Browne, Viscount Castlerosse, he became the Earl of Kenmore. We're divorced now. So I became Viscountess Castlerosse.'

Von Brummer didn't begin to understand the English aristocracy, the swathes, the tiers of them, or the English class system. So he nodded his head as if he did.

She smiled briefly again, then slowly uncrossed her leg.

'They can take your good name,' she said slowly, 'but they can't take your title.'

He nodded again. Understandingly, he hoped.

'So, Doris, what is this about? What has the picture to do with it.'

'It's proof of my bona fides. You can check me out, I'm sure, if you don't believe my story. No doubt there are several nobles and earls you can confirm with and who are anxious to talk to you. I can give you a list if you like.'

She looked away from him and to the portrait propped up on the chair. 'I never cared for it too much. I just posed for it to please Winston. It kept him occupied. Well, he seemed to enjoy it.'

'Forgive me if this sounds brusque, but did you have an affair?'

'An affair?' she paused as if weighing it up. 'Others would probably call it that. It was a dalliance.'

That bitter smile again. 'A repeated dalliance. He wasn't much up to any commitment, it wouldn't so much have ruined him in society as scuppered his political career. You know, cited as co-respondent in a divorce action would have finished that off.'

'So it wasn't just in France?'

'Oh no, he'd pop round to the house in Devonshire Gardens, giving advance notice of course so I could give the servants the evening off. It suited both of us. He could be quite charming too. But like Val, my husband, totally hopeless in bed. Although he did say to me at the Ritz in Paris, "Doris, you could make a corpse come".'

Mueller coughed and hoped his face wasn't colouring. 'How did it suit you, Doris?'

'Hmm, well I could see he was on his way up, he introduced me to many important people, Val did too, of course, connections. They're so important don't you think?'

Mueller considered this and nodded. 'So does this bring us up to date? You are seeking another connection.'

She smiled without warmth once more. 'Well let me just put it this way, mine have loosened considerably since the divorce.'

'You are, how is it put, hard up?'

A slight nod of the head. 'I've had to sell all my jewellery. I was in New York, it didn't end too well. Winston was meant to send me the fare to return, but he didn't. He has never been generous.'

Perhaps occupied with more pressing matters, Mueller thought. Winning a war.

'Not quite impoverished,' she added, 'but not living in the way I'm accustomed to. And I'll never see my diamonds again.'

'And you are here because you think that Churchill let you down and I can help you become accustomed again. That and revenge on him for spurning you?'

'Well…Y-e-s-s,' she pursed lip, 'more or less.'

'And why should I?'

This time the laugh was genuine as she threw back her head, the curls on her cheeks quivering. 'Because I can find Winston for you.'

For a few seconds von Brummer said nothing as the words lodged in his brain. He tried to damp down the swell of excitement he felt and maintain what he hoped was his sombre consideration.

'How do you know,' he measured out the words, 'that he isn't dead?'

Doris slowly shook her head, as if she was dismissing an infantile remark. 'If he was you wouldn't be asking that, now would you?'

And she sat back on the sofa and crossed her legs once more.

'And how would you go about finding Churchill if he were alive.'

'I said my connections had loosened. Not severed.'

Mueller eased off the desk, clasped his hands behind his back and walked over to the armchair, staring down at the portrait.

'It doesn't do you justice, Doris.'

'Thank you. Frankly, I would have sold it in the past if I had found anyone in the least interested.'

Mueller turned round. 'There's much here for me to consider and I really have to attend a meeting shortly. I suggest we continue this discussion over dinner. How does that sound?'

He smiled at her. 'It will also give me time to check out one or two matters. What do you say?'

Doris stood up. 'That sounds excellent.'

'I'm not well informed about London restaurants. Can you recommend one?' he said.

'I've always enjoyed Rules in Covent Garden, but I'm not sure if it's open.'

Mueller took her hand in both of his. 'If it isn't, it shall be. I will send a car for you at 7pm. My secretary Fiona will arrange it if you give her the address to collect you from. I look forward to it.' His head snapped forward and he leaned over and kissed her hand more forcefully this time.

16

Coogan's life had been a series of coincidences, like everyone else's he supposed. He couldn't help thinking about it as he drove through the night. It was almost as if he had to sum up his life so far, whether it had been well lived, because he wasn't convinced there was too much of it left.

He had been born in Moodiesburn, about eight miles north-east of Glasgow, but he had left, been taken by his mother, when he was five or six, he couldn't remember the year for sure. But he did recall briefly attending primary school for a few months, where the tawse, the thick leather belt, seemed to rule, slapping the fear of failing to gain knowledge into children.

All he could remember about his father was his back, as he sat in the tin bath in front of the fire, pockmarked with dark spots, which he realised later were coal chips punched in over the years from scrabbling throughout the narrow seams in the mine. It was the Auchengeich colliery, he knew, from his mother, one of the few things she'd admit to about his Dad.

It was unusual for women to leave husbands then, it was now too, so the abuse must have been substantial. And it required enormous courage. All she would say about it was 'he was not a good man,' in her lilting Dublin accent.

He knew that there had been another child, an earlier one, a brother, who had died in childbirth. He was lucky he guessed, although it didn't seem like it now. She was dressmaker, Agnes, his Ma, working from home, although that was a rather extravagant description of it. It was a single-end, just the one room, in a tenement in Springburn, with a recess where the bed was, curtains drawn across it during the day, the toilet on the half landing, shared with three other families. 'So the seat was almost warm,' she said about it, smiling.

She worked at the sewing machine on the table in the middle of the small room from early in the morning until he went to the bed, it seemed, although that clearly wasn't the case, because she still made time to feed him – she did the shopping, the messages as they called it, also of course. And the washing in the communal steamie in the back court. He remembered the mud all around, the rats, one of the games was trying to kill them with bricks and stones. It rarely produced a result.

In the late evening, for an hour or so, she'd listen to the radio and read in front of the small, coal-fired range where she cooked. How she got time to go to the library he didn't know, but she was buried in a new book every week and not sloppy romances, but serious fiction, classics. That's where his love of books and literature came from. He hadn't been able to pursue that at school, he had to leave at fourteen and take up an apprenticeship like all the others. He was lucky, or so he was told, that she knew someone working at NB Loco just up the road and that's where he started, as a machinist.

The end came very quickly. She had been coughing for several weeks and although he kept urging her to go to the doctor she always said she couldn't afford to. It was a Friday, he came back with his intact pay packet and she was lying barely conscious in the bed. He ran to the doctor, threatened he'd break him if he didn't come now, and she didn't last the night. He sat beside the bed as are breath slowly gave out, with a final death rattle.

He was almost nineteen, newly out of his apprenticeship, he paid the undertaker and then caught the first bus going south, wanting to get as far away as possible.

Now, hitting the first road block, twenty miles out of Birmingham, stopped his reverie. There were three of them, men twice his age, two with shotguns, the third with a heavy revolver. He talked his way through it, news of the blowing up of the armaments factory had reached them. He told them he was going to Liverpool looking for work, someone he knew said he might get a job at the docks, and after fifteen minutes or so they let him go.

The second road block was around ten miles out of the city – by now he was shivering, although it was as mild evening, well early morning now, from the winds he had ridden into over the previous eighty miles or so – but his interrogation was cut short when the sky above was cut through with searchlights, against puffs of grey smoke from anti-aircraft fire. He watched three German bombers picked out by the lights, and then what was surely a Spitfire or a Hurricane join in. One of the enemy planes, clearly hit, spiralled away and down until he lost sight of it, and then the far-off sound of the explosion as it hit the ground, he hoped in open ground, the flare of red over the horizon. He lost sight of the other planes, but then there were several rapid crumps of noise which he guessed were discarded bombs.

That's when he kicked the BSA into life again and roared off towards it all.

It took him an hour and stopping to ask several people for directions before he got to the address in Bootle he had memorised. He was several hours too late. All that was standing in the street was a small church, and even that was scarred with bomb damage, windows blown out, the cross on the roof hanging brokenly, defeated. Most of the street was smoking rubble, dozens of people, ARP wardens, several police officers and local people, some still in night clothes, pulling at the stones and beams looking for survivors. A knot of women stood watching, crying, clutching each other. He turned the bike and headed for the docks.

It was evident that they had been the main target, he could see that from the damage, although it looked mostly superficial. The Cunard building had all its windows blown out with damage to the roof. The streets leading up to it had also been hit, up to mile or more away he noticed as he had made his way, weaving past bricks and rubble on the roads to the waterfront.

A light rain had come on. The air smelled of burned anthracite with occasional whiffs of petrol. He wondered how many had been killed, sitting on his bike on the cobbled street looking towards the jungle of masts and funnels from the ships moored along the long wharves. None of them looked as if they had been hit. Only the civilians had suffered. He thought of the fighter pilot who had taken on the three enemy bombers – why just three, had others in the flight been brought down earlier? – who had probably saved the docks.

'Excuse me,' he said to a man in dark overalls sweeping glass from the street behind him, 'I need to go to Dublin.'

The man looked up, pushed the brim of his cap back. 'Well you won't get there on that.'

Coogan nodded his head, taking part in the joke. 'I'm not much of a swimmer either.'

'The B&I ferry, if it's still running. That's what you want.'

The cleaner was leaning on his brush now, probably thankful for an excuse to break from the brushing.

'B&I?'

'It's Sunday name is the British and Irish Steam Packet Company. You'll find the office further along there,' he pointed with his spare hand. 'If it's open.'

Coogan thanked him, put the bike into gear and moved off along the street, chugging several hundred yards to the office. Which was closed. He didn't know what time it was, but it was bright now, although still early. It was just a matter of waiting. He had nothing else to do.

And if it didn't open?

He didn't want to think about that.

Instead he thought of Fleur and wondered once again where she was, if she had gone back to Brittany. She had always been independent, well in his experience, and it wasn't any real surprise that she should make her own decision about returning to France.

'I have to go. I hope you understand?'

He didn't, but he nodded.

'When it's over we'll meet again,' he said.

'Of course we will, my love.'

Although neither of them believed it.

'Here,' he had said, 'take this.' He rummaged in his pocket. 'It was my mother's.'

She looked down a his open palm and what he was holding.

'A ring? Is that you proposing?'

'It was her wedding ring. She never wore it. I found it in a drawer after she died. When it's over. If you'll have me.'

She smiled, leaned forward and kissed him.

'I suppose you'll do,' she said, then kissed him again.

There would be other kisses before she left, but that was the decisive one.

He came out of the past when he heard the clank of shutters and saw a woman pulling them open from the windows of the B&I offices.

'I need a ticket to Dublin,' he said urgently as crossed the step into the small office.

The woman, a girl really, shrugged. 'You're lucky,' she said across the counter. 'Perhaps.'

She smiled at him, he thought rather sadly. She didn't look more than sixteen, her hair cut short almost like a boy's, a mole on her right cheek on her thin, chiselled face.

'There's a sailing at 11am. It could be the last one. There's talk of her being requisitioned. The ship. MV Munster.'

He glanced at the clock on the wall above the board with the timetables pinned to it. Eight-thirty.

'I hope I am. Lucky.'

Now they were almost an hour out from Liverpool. Coogan could still see the outline of the land behind as he leaned on the rail on the stern of the ship. He had given up everything, the rented house he had shared with Fleur, the bike left on the quay for someone to take away, and it didn't matter. None of it. What mattered was the future.

He took out the framed photograph of her he had brought with him. There was a crack in the glass now. He wondered if there would ever be any more and whether this was all of her he would ever have of her. A shiver, perhaps of sadness, shook him. No, he would find her. He had to think that.

He looked at her, looking back at him, she was so beautiful. She knew that but she didn't care about it, it wasn't important, she just laughed off compliments. Sure of herself.

He remembered the first time he untied her hair and it fell to her shoulders and how it looked, a shimmering, dark amber glow against her naked skin in the half-light.

Then he put the photograph back in his jacket pocket and went inside.